By: Ben Herr

**WARNING**

This series conveys strong messages about gender equality and social justice. There are also elements of the unseen, magic, and spirituality.

Alynia Sky, The Beginning and the End

Copyright © 2013 Benjamin Joseph Herr

Exterior art by Stephanie Anderson, Danny Simanjaya, and Jennifer Harris

www.AlyniaSky.com

First Edition

0 9 8 7 6 5 4 3 2 1

What can one girl do?

Anything, if she is *empowered*!

This book is dedicated to all the women who guided me, loved me, and offered me friendship. Thank you for enchanting my life and making my soul smile.

In the mystic time of autumn, the gemstones are found, and the Valkyries fly free.

# Contents

# Chapter 1

## Racing to Red Rock River

Every morning, the Sun awoke and began his slow ascent over the great continent of Ka'lanna, banishing the night sky and the darkness that had unleashed themselves across the land in his absence. As the Sun's golden beams fanned from the eastern horizon, all forms of life began to stir and awaken from their slumbers. Sunlight began to warm the villages of humankind, and the people of the world faced the new day with the warmth of their star shining down upon them. Once the Sun made his way halfway through the sky above Ka'lanna, he would slow his daily journey, coming almost to a stop. The rolling hills, grassy plains, and woodlands all danced in harmony, bathing in the warmth and the light.

The Goodwind tribe lived at the mystic intersection where all the terrains blended together and became one land. They were the only humans who still honored the blessed ways of Sehebre. When the Sun reached the outskirts of their village most of them still slept, but the early risers awaited each morning silently in anticipation, for the ones who guarded the nighttime fires had recently surrendered to slumber. The early risers stood frozen in a meditative stance, almost as if they had removed themselves from time. In their minds they imagined themselves as beaming balls of light, sending their love to everyone they cared about; everyone they hoped to protect from the plague of duality.

The sunbeams kissed the animals inhabiting the wood, darting along, dancing in the forest, creating light, and casting out shadows. The animals marveled as the flowers instantly bloomed when touched by the powerful light. Tribe members slowly awoke from their meditative states, taking in the wonderful and fresh smells of a new day. Bright green grass shimmered as the dew of the night before evaporated. The new day had officially begun for humans and animals alike.

Crisp fragrances drifted in the wind. The Sun finished passing over the rolling hills, moving up and down between all the spaces and caves, causing the last of the darkness to flee. By this time most of the other tribe members were awake and slowly beginning their day, all were waiting the magical moment when the light reached the highest point in the area, a place known as Sehebre's Finger. Once the new day's light found this point, it burst across the valley, reflecting like an immense galactic waterfall, spilling its warmth and brightness across the sky, igniting the entire village in a mirage of golden flames. With all his glory the Sun shined brightly over the village of the Goodwind tribe, blessing them for honoring the ways of Sehebre.

Only one hut in the village was constructed so its entrance faced Sehebre's Finger. This hut was the home of Nabu, the tribe's oldest shaman. Time had been gentle to the revered shaman, who didn't have a single wrinkle on his face. Had he not kept it shaved, his hair would have flown out like stars spilling from the Milky Way in golden abundance, as many young tribe members chose to wear theirs.

Nabu was the most versed and practiced in the ancient ways, and with his great powers, he had led the tribe through many harsh times. Many tribe members believed that the universe was on his side, because repeatedly, through many tribulations, his advice and predictions had come true.

Every morning, Nabu waited for the shower of light that came down from the Sun, striking Sehebre's Finger, when he would quickly rise and begin his morning routine. With sleep still in his eyes, he smudged the remnants of burned sage leaves in

8

a hollow turtle shell, adding rosemary he had harvested from the nearby fields. When lavender was available, he added it to this mixture. Once the ingredients were thoroughly mixed, he added the most sacred ingredient—water from the last rainfall.

Nabu sat in meditation and prayer while holding this herbal potion. After he finished his morning prayers, he quietly went through the village blessing all the huts of his fellow tribesmen. He stood in front of each hut, gently dipping his fingers into the turtle shell and then casting a small amount of the magic elixir onto each hut. As he did this, he chanted the words "Shanti, Shanti, Shanti, Namay Namay, ya Namay oh Seh Taulgh Namay." During this ceremony, he was careful not to awaken any tribespeople who might be sleeping late, especially the ones who remained awake at night to guard the fires.

Nabu did not know that every morning, even though he tried to keep quiet, he managed to awaken a lone rooster named Frumpy, who enjoyed sleeping late into the day, far past the time the other village roosters rose. As Nabu made his third pass around the village, the leaves Frumpy used as a bed began to rustle, just as they had every day for years. Frumpy fluffed his spotted feathers, slowly starting to wake, shaking his head to clear the scent of the sacred herbal concoction Nabu cast in the air. Frumpy hated the smell of rosemary, but the smell of burned sage bothered him the most. It disgusted him so much that he tried to hold his breath for as long as he could, wishing that, this day, Nabu would finally stop his incantations, and the smell would be gone forever.

Frumpy had to take a breath and as soon as he did, the sickening smell overtook him, and he knew that he was up for the day. He rose from his bed and scowled at Nabu, waiting for the shaman to finish his blessings and head to the Northern Woods.

Once Nabu left the village, Frumpy waited a few minutes for the air to clear. He clamped his beak with his wings and began to wobble from his pile of leaves behind the hut of O'stara and Nak'te toward the front entrance of their home. A young girl, the daughter of O'stara and Nak'te, lived in the hut, and she was Frumpy's best friend. Her name was Alynia Sky.

9

Alynia Sky was taller than average for her thirteen years with long, dark hair that flowed and shone in the sunlight. Frumpy adored the way the light cascaded from her hair. It reminded him of the times he'd been awake when the sunlight first burst forth over the hills and caused the light show that awoke the village every day by striking Sehebre's Finger.

Alynia was strong and adventurous, and her grown-up friends called her a daring dreamer, but she wasn't sure if she believed them. She wondered if they were just finding a nice way of saying that she was always getting in trouble. There weren't any other children her age in the village, so she got bored often, which usually led to trouble. Frumpy had taken to her almost immediately when they met, and they'd started sneaking out almost every morning to fish together at a nearby stream.

Frumpy carefully pushed the bearskin door covering to the side, peering into the smoky darkness of Alynia's home. He discovered that Alynia and her parents were still sleeping! He puffed out his chest. People sleeping later than he? Absurd!

"Alynia," he whispered, but she only rolled over and turned her back to him.

"Alynia, wake up!" he exclaimed.

This time, Alynia's eyes opened, and she jerked upright, startled. She looked around the room, confused, but then she saw Frumpy peek his head into the room through the doorway. A few rays of light came in the door where he had pushed the bearskin to the side, illuminating his head feathers and causing them to glow as if he had a halo.

Alynia smiled at Frumpy. "Hey, glowworm head," she said, which made him scowl. "I'll be out in a minute."

Frumpy pulled his head back, and the hut was completely dark again. Alynia quietly rose from her bed and stood in the darkness for a moment, stretching her stiff muscles, preparing for whatever adventures would come her way. She threw on a light coat and began to sneak toward the door as quietly as she could, so she wouldn't wake her parents. Her parents were night watchers, meaning that their jobs were to stay awake with the moon and the owls, making sure that the

10

village fires stayed lit and that nothing bad happened in the night. Alynia knew it was important for them to sleep later in the day than most people.

When she neared the door, Alynia took one of her father's fishing spears and pushed the bearskin aside as quietly as possible. When she did this, the sunlight reentered and spilled across her mother's face, causing her to wake. O'stara smiled at her only daughter as she placed her finger over her lips, signaling Alynia to be quiet so her father wouldn't wake.

"I love you, daughter," O'stara whispered. O'stara was proud of Alynia for being such an adventurer, but Nak'te was not as understanding. Nak'te wanted Alynia to study under Nabu and learn the ways of the ancient shaman. He couldn't understand why she spent all her free time hanging out with the silly bird Frumpy, sitting idly by a river or, just as often, getting into trouble.

Alynia winked at her mother, making sure that her father was still snoring, and then stepped out of the hut.

"Good morning, Frumpy," she said, smiling enthusiastically and stretching her arms toward the sky. It was going to be a beautiful day.

"Good morning to you, my lady," Frumpy replied, bowing theatrically.

Alynia looked around in every direction, searching to make sure that no one was watching who would disapprove of her avoiding her chores to spend time with her friend.

"Are you sure that Nabu is gone?" she asked. "Is everyone else already working on their chores for the day?"

"That nasty smell of sage and rosemary is almost gone," Frumpy replied, expressing his displeasure. "So, he must be."

Alynia giggled at Frumpy as he made an exaggerated gesture of covering his beak with both his wings. He then fell to the ground, sticking his tongue out of his mouth, pretending to be dead. Frumpy always had the best jokes.

11

After another moment of this, he looked up at Alynia and asked her if she'd like to race to the Red Rock River. She nodded her head, excited at the prospect. They began to sneak between huts, making their way to the woods on the western side of the village.

"Are you ready?" Alynia asked as they reached the village border. "You know that I'm going to..."

She didn't finish her sentence, because Frumpy had already taken off, and once she started to run herself, he was already ahead of her by at least fifty feet. She ran as quickly as she could, her feet digging into the dirt, kicking up clouds of dust behind her as she slowly gained on Frumpy.

He tried to pick up his pace, but having short and stumpy rooster legs proved a disadvantage. He put as much effort as he could into speeding up, but he'd sadly used most of his energy on getting the head start at the beginning of the race. Only a moment later, Alynia passed him, and he noticed that she wasn't even sweating as she effortlessly called to him.

"I'll see you at the twisted tree!" she exclaimed, waving to him as she rounded a sharp turn a short way ahead of him. After that, she was out of sight.

Once Frumpy made his way to the turn, the only way he knew that she'd been there was by the dust settling out of the air around him. He slowed down after that, because he knew that he wouldn't win the race today.

"Tomorrow, I'll get an even bigger head start," he promised himself.

Alynia arrived at the twisted tree, reaching out to touch it first and officially signal that she'd won the competition. She turned to look back on the path she'd raced on but couldn't see Frumpy anywhere. She knew that he was probably walking now, just as he did almost every time they raced. One day, she would let him win, just to see the look on his face. She sat down in the shade of the old gnarled tree, reaching into her bag. She pulled out an ear of roasted corn, still in the husk, and began to shuck it. Just as she was about to take her first bite of breakfast, she heard a voice.

"Did you bring any for me?"

Alynia looked in the voice's direction. A few yards away on the bank of the Red Rock River, she saw her friend Swiftfeather.

"Swiftfeather!" Alynia exclaimed. "I didn't see you there!"

Swiftfeather was a young hawk with a generous spirit, but he also had a stern, no-nonsense disposition, especially when he was hungry. He was one of the first orphans raised by Tenderheart in the branches of the nearby willow, and he'd lived at Red Rock River for almost five years. Although he was old enough to move away and live on his own, he chose to stay and help with the young orphans Tenderheart took into her home.

Swiftfeather flew over from the riverbank and landed next to Alynia, feathers glistening with droplets of river water reflected by the sunlight.

"So, is that for me, or what?" he repeated himself.

"If Frumpy doesn't get here soon, you can have his," she said, reaching into her bag for another ear of roasted corn. "It's still warm from the fire."

"No!" they heard Frumpy cry out in the distance, obviously distressed by this turn of events. "No, he can't!"

Alynia and Swiftfeather both looked down the path and saw Frumpy scurrying as fast as he could on his short legs, trying to make it to the twisted tree in time to save his breakfast.

"It's no big deal, Frumpy," Swiftfeather taunted. "I don't even like corn."

"That's nice to know!" Frumpy retorted, snatching the second ear of corn out of Alynia's hand.

Alynia scowled at her rooster friend. "You're welcome, Frumpy!" she huffed. "But you should mind your manners!"

"Let him have all the corn," Swiftfeather said. "I've already caught more than fifteen fish today."

13

"Were you having trouble sleeping again?" Alynia asked as she squinted to see Swiftfeather's basket of fish on the opposite bank of the river.

"More and more orphans are brought out to the willow every day," he sighed. "It's hard to share the tree with that many nestlings sometimes. You should try it yourself!"

Alynia laughed. "I'd definitely fall out of a tree the moment I tried to sleep, but if you want, you can stay in the village with us. Nabu really likes hawks."

"I wish he liked roosters enough to stop spreading that wretched stench all over the village every morning," Frumpy added.

Alynia silently glared at Frumpy. Her stare was intense enough to cause him to lower his head in shame for insulting the ancient ways of Nabu.

Swiftfeather shrugged. "Maybe I'll just take a vacation. Anyway, I have enough fish for everyone, so you don't have to spear any today... unless you just want to practice. If so, I will help."

Alynia agreed that she could use some practice, and she enjoyed fishing, so she picked up her father's spear and walked over to the riverbank. She silently watched the river flow past her, being as still as she could. She moved her eyes back and forth across the waters, following the flows and currents, searching for her prey. After several moments passed, she hurled the spear high in the air. The three friends watched as it flew up and then curved back down, splashing into the waters halfway across the river. Alynia began to wade into the water, heading toward the spear as it slowly drifted in the river.

Swiftfeather and Frumpy watched from the shore.

"Alynia, be careful! You don't know how to swim!" Frumpy called out, reminding her of the time she had gone too deep in a pond near the village, and her father had jumped in the water to save her. She shivered thinking of the waters going over her head, but she was determined to remain brave and not look frightened in front of her friends.

14

"It's only up to my waist," she answered, pulling the spear out of the water. The birds watched in amazement as she plucked a large, gasping fish from the razor-sharp tip of the spear.

"You can add this one to the pile," she told Swiftfeather.

Laughing, he replied, "I guess you won't need any more lessons from me with a trick like that!"

She made her way to the shore across the river. "It's no big deal. Maybe a few more lessons will help me," she yelled over the sound of the waters, tossing the fish into the basket of fish that Swiftfeather had started filling earlier.

She paused for a moment, and then called to them again. "Come on, guys; let's go see Tenderheart." She motioned for her friends to follow her by crossing the river. While she waited on them to cross, she began to wring the water out of her clothes, which were completely drenched from the splashes she'd made crossing all the way over. Once her clothes were wrung out, she struggled to lift the basket of fish. It was so heavy! Frumpy and Swiftfeather finished crossing the river and rushed over to help Alynia with the basket.

"I guess this one's going on my back?" Frumpy asked as he knelt down next to the basket. Alynia leaned the basket, balancing it on one side as Frumpy crawled under it.

"Are you sure you have it?" Alynia asked.

"I may not win the race, but I'm definitely strong," Frumpy reassured her.

"Just in case, I'll help you out," Swiftfeather volunteered, flying up and attaching his talons to the rim of the basket while flapping his wings.

Alynia helped maintain the basket's balance as they began to walk toward the willow where Tenderheart and all the orphans lived. The basket occasionally wobbled, and they'd have a scare as they worried about the fish tumbling out of it and falling all over the ground. It didn't help that some fish were still alive in the basket and flailing!

15

No path on the side of the shore led to the great willow, because most members of the Goodwind tribe had no need to cross the river. The tribe's ceremonies were usually held in the northlands, and their hunting had been most prosperous in the lands south of the village. Most residents of the willow could fly, so they didn't need a path in the first place.

The three friends made good progress toward the willow, even with the heavy load they carried. When they were about halfway to the tree, Swiftfeather suddenly let go of the rim of the basket and flew up in the air causing Frumpy to let out a cry of pain because he didn't expect the full weight of the basket with all the fish to come down on his back. Alynia immediately tried to shift the weight of the basket off her friend who squawked as if he were being crushed alive. In trying to get the weight readjusted, they accidentally tipped the basket too far, and most fish spilled on the ground.

"Are you OK?" Alynia asked, helping Frumpy off the ground where he'd melodramatically collapsed.

He didn't respond for a moment, walking in a circle around the basket while fluffing out his chest feathers.

"I'll be OK," he scowled, "but what about these fish?" He pointed his wing at all the fish scattered on the ground around them.

"They'll be fine. We can wash them before we feed them to the orphans," Alynia reassured him, deciding not to make fun of him for bragging about how strong he was earlier. She knew it would upset him more if she joked about it, so she saved it for later when he could take the joke better. They began to gather the fish and place them back in the basket.

When they had all the fish back in the basket, Frumpy began to scan the air above them, searching for Swiftfeather, ready to deliver some harsh words about the hawk's sudden flight and its disastrous results. Then, he spotted something.

"Alynia, look up!" Frumpy cried, pointing directly above them, jabbing at the air.

Alynia looked into the clear blue sky until she spotted the hawk circling high above them. *What's he doing?* she thought. A few seconds later, she noticed that a second hawk was swooping around Swiftfeather. She stared at the second hawk and realized that he was carrying a basket of his own. She squinted, trying to identify him by the markings of his feathers, but she couldn't recognize who he was. The two hawks continued circling above them, getting lower and closer to the ground with each pass they made.

Finally, Swiftfeather landed a few yards away from Alynia and Frumpy. Frumpy immediately dashed off toward Swiftfeather, ready to give him a piece of his mind. Just as he began to yell at his friend, the second hawk landed between the two, blocking Frumpy's route.

Alynia walked toward the group of birds, intrigued by the second hawk. She looked closely at the new arrival, but she knew for sure that she'd never met him before. She soon realized that she'd been mistaken about the hawk carrying a basket. It was actually a nest! The hawk's gray spots and the nest he was carrying fascinated Alynia.

"Alynia!" Swiftfeather shouted as she stepped closer to him. His voice broke through her fascinated trance, and she shifted her focus away from the nest. She was sure she saw something moving in it, but her attention was diverted to Swiftfeather.

"Alynia. Frumpy. This is Greyspot of the Far North." Swiftfeather introduced them to the hawk.

Greyspot cleared his throat, and then spoke in a calm yet commanding voice. "I've traveled a great distance from the lands of the North in search of the falcon known as Tenderheart. I know that I'm close but am ashamed to admit that I've become somewhat lost. Your friend Swiftfeather explained that you're on your way there now. If it pleases you, I'd like to travel with you the rest of the way there."

Greyspot had captured Alynia's undivided attention. She continued to stare at him, and he stared back, equally interested in her.

"Do I know you, little girl?" Greyspot asked, tilting his head.

She didn't directly answer his question, introducing herself and her rooster friend.

"I'm Alynia, and this is my friend Frumpy. You've already met Swiftfeather. I think it would be wonderful if you chose to travel with us."

Greyspot asked her another question, one that seemed random to her. "Do yellow flowers mean anything to you, Alynia?"

Alynia locked eyes with Greyspot as she searched for any particular memories or meanings concerning yellow flowers, but none came to mind. "I like how they smell," she answered.

"Oh, never mind, then." Greyspot shook his head, chuckling. "I'm sure I've mistaken you for someone else."

"I'm really curious about the nest you're carrying," Alynia said. "I thought I saw something moving in it."

"Indeed, you did. You have good eyes, young one," Greyspot replied. "I'm taking an orphaned songbird to Tenderheart at the willow with great hopes that she will be able to care for it."

Alynia knelt down beside the nest. Greyspot fluffed his feathers a bit, checking with Swiftfeather to make sure that she wouldn't harm the young bird in the nest. Swiftfeather nodded his approval.

"Come on out, little one," Alynia cooed, tapping the ground next to the nest. A moment passed, and then a small black bird with a yellow chest poked its head out of the nest. The young bird had a frightened look in its eyes, and it shook with nervousness. Frumpy, tired of being excluded from the conversation, rushed toward the little bird, intending to say hello but instead causing the little bird to retreat into the nest.

Alynia scolded Frumpy and then resumed her efforts at coaxing the baby back into the open.

18

"His name is Poplin," Greyspot whispered.

"Hi there, little Poplin," Alynia smiled. "I'm Alynia. We're going to help you get to Tenderheart's willow. She's the best at taking care of birds like you." She extended her hand toward the nest, and to everyone's surprise, little Poplin hopped out and onto Alynia's hand.

"He likes you!" exclaimed Frumpy.

Alynia lifted Poplin up to her shoulder, gazing at him with loving eyes. "I like him too!" she stated, stroking his feathers. Poplin began to whistle a quiet, happy song as he rested on her shoulder, nuzzling against her neck and hair.

Swiftfeather made his way to the basket of fish that they were taking to the tree.

"Greyspot, it looks like Poplin will go the rest of the way with Alynia. Can you help me with this basket? I'm afraid it's just too much for my friend to carry the rest of the way." Swiftfeather winked at Alynia.

"I can do it! I just lost my balance!" Frumpy defended himself.

"I don't mind helping you," Greyspot answered, joining Swiftfeather. Together, the two hawks lifted the basket in the air as they headed toward Tenderheart's willow.

Alynia was so preoccupied with her newest friend that she didn't even notice that they'd flown off. Standing a few steps behind her, Frumpy sulked a little, occasionally letting out exasperated and exaggerated sighs of discontent.

After a few minutes Alynia, Poplin, and Frumpy, continued towards the willow tree. By this time Swiftfeather, Greyspot, and the basket of fish were nothing more than a speck in the sky. All the friends were finally on their way to Tenderheart's.

19

# Chapter 2

## On the Way to Tenderheart's Willow

Alynia continued to walk through the woods to the west of Red Rock River, steadily making her way toward Tenderheart's willow. Her new friend Poplin had discovered a comfortable spot on her shoulder and had perched there. His spirits were raised by the marvelous stories she told him about the new life he would have once they arrived at the willow, and he was nervous and excited about meeting all the other orphans there. Every few minutes, Alynia paused, looking over her shoulder, making sure that Frumpy was keeping up.

"Thanks for waiting for me," Frumpy clucked, out of breath. The race with Alynia earlier in the morning had really worn him out! If only he'd been able to sleep in a little later, he wouldn't have been so exhausted this early in the day, he thought.

"Friends don't leave friends behind," Alynia reminded him as she patted him on the head and then continued to make her way through the dense and luscious woodland.

"Would you tell me more about Tenderheart?" Poplin inquired.

"You'll have to wait and see," Alynia replied, pointing in front of them. "We're almost there!"

Down the path was a small clearing in the forest. Tenderheart's willow stood in the center of the clearing. Poplin had to squint his young eyes, but from what he could make out of the willow, it seemed glorious. He'd been frightened about not having a true home since Greyspot rescued him, and as they grew closer to the willow, the orphanage seemed more and more like a sanctuary.

He stared in awe at the massive fifty-foot branches that arched out from the trunk and bent toward the ground. He was very curious about the other birds he saw bouncing from limb to limb of the tree, and he wondered whether they'd like him and what songs he would learn to sing there. The tree branches sparkled with dew, and the brilliant greens of the leaves and earthy browns of the tree's bark were inviting as the sunlight came down and warmed the clearing. They hadn't passed a single tree in the entire forest that had the alluring presence of the willow in the whole time they'd traveled from Red Rock River.

A breeze came through the forest as they approached Tenderheart's orphanage, and as it swept past the friends, it seemed to carry away all Poplin's worries and sadness, lifting his little heart as if it floated through his chest. He wondered whether the tree was magical, because he'd never felt happiness like that in his young life.

Alynia moved forward with Poplin still sitting on her shoulder and approached the great willow. "Go ahead and jump up," Alynia encouraged him, taking him in her hand and holding him as high as she could reach.

Poplin looked at Alynia nervously. "Is this really going to be my new home?" he asked, afraid to believe in something too good to be true.

Alynia smiled at him as the wind blew through the willow branches. The branches skimmed across both Alynia and Poplin, brushing them as they swayed.

"Watch this," Alynia said, placing him back on her shoulder, then slowly extending her arms forward and parting them out to the sides. She took another step forward with Poplin chirping nervously, and then they passed into the secret world hidden in the blanket of the willow's branches.

21

Poplin couldn't believe his eyes. He began to twitter in astonishment, fluttering his wings and hopping on Alynia's shoulder. He couldn't believe that everything he suddenly saw was tucked away in the willow branches, hidden from the outside world. The sun seemed to shine from every direction at once, and everything seemed to glow, as if some magical haze had been cast over all the branches around them.

Several thick vines hung down from every branch, and on all the vines, there were many clusters of nests of different shapes and sizes. All around them, birds sang and chirped, flying back and forth, playing games with one another.

Poplin was unsure where to focus his attention. The birds learning to hunt intrigued him. The singing classes on another branch also looked like something of which he wanted to be part. He saw birds learning how to build nests, birds playing hide-and-seek, and he even saw one group of birds jumping off their branch with what seemed like parachutes. Those birds were very young, so maybe they were learning to fly for the first time. Poplin wasn't that great at flying himself, so he made a mental note to ask about that group later. Every bird he saw seemed full of life and vigor, but most notably, every bird in the branches seemed happy.

"Thank you! Thank you!" Poplin cried as he marveled at the scenes before him.

A mountain of baskets at the base of the tree caught his eye. The baskets were filled to the brim with all sorts of delicious foods—fish, berries, and all types of seeds. The lovely aroma of the feast made Poplin's stomach growl. He gazed up, following the tree trunk toward the sky, where he saw a small opening in the tree that seemed carved out long ago by a woodpecker. A glorious falcon sat in the hollow crevice, staring down at Poplin and Alynia. The falcon was old and majestic, and her eyes sparkled with wit and wisdom. Her white feathers were as bright as the sun, and it seemed to Poplin that the glowing aura that radiated from everything inside this hidden world was a result of her presence there.

Alynia stepped toward the falcon, bowing slightly, and then took Poplin off her shoulder and back into her hands. She

22

cupped him in both hands and offered him up, presenting him to the wise old falcon. The falcon didn't speak, but tilted her head from side to side, examining the small songbird and his yellow spots. Poplin tried to be brave, although the falcon intimidated him, and he puffed out his chest as far as he could to seem bigger than he really was.

"What a lovely little songbird you've brought me," the falcon finally spoke. "He'll make a delicious dinner!"

Poplin's eyes widened, and he backed away from the falcon as much as he could, still cupped in Alynia's hands. The falcon then laughed the cheeriest and happiest laugh Poplin had ever heard. He felt relief when he realized that the falcon was only joking.

"Welcome to your new home, youngling," said the falcon, looking down at Poplin with wide, loving eyes. "You may call me Tenderheart. This is my orphanage."

"Thank you for letting me stay here," Poplin answered humbly.

Tenderheart whistled loudly, getting the attention of many nearby birds. "Everyone!" she announced. "You have a new brother! Little bird, introduce yourself!"

Poplin was more nervous than ever. Everyone was staring at him.

He cleared his throat. "I'm Poplin," he began, but a loud birdcall from the branches high above interrupted him. It was Swiftfeather!

Swiftfeather swooped down and landed on a branch near Poplin, Tenderheart, Alynia, and Frumpy, who'd remained unusually silent in the presence of Tenderheart.

"Little Poplin's from the Far North, but he doesn't know how to fly very well," Swiftfeather announced. "Everyone, do your best to help him while he adjusts to living here!"

Tenderheart smiled at Swiftfeather.

"Please show your new brother around," she requested. "Your job is to protect him and help him."

Swiftfeather fluttered into the air and flew over toward Poplin and Alynia, scooping Poplin up in his talons, and then returning to the branch from which he'd launched. He ushered Poplin toward a nearby nest that several other small birds were peeking out of timidly.

"Alynia, please follow me," Tenderheart asked, and then flew up toward the highest part of the tree. Alynia began to climb the tree as quickly as she could. She knew that she wasn't the best or swiftest climber, but she made it to the top quickly because she had climbed the willow many times before. The willow branches gently brushed Alynia as she peered through them once she had climbed as high as she could.

"Have you been studying?" Tenderheart asked.

Still holding on with both hands because of how high she was, Alynia shrugged. "A little," she answered, looking out at the sky around them, watching as the afternoon blue slowly slipped away. Alynia had failed to realize how much time she and the others had spent, as her father would put it, sitting idly by a river. Early evening was approaching, and the Sun was heading for the horizon. A few stars had broken through the Sun's veil and began to twinkle in the twilight sky.

"Which constellation is ruling?" Tenderheart asked.

"Orvieto," Alynia confidently answered.

"Excellent," said Tenderheart. "Which constellation will Orvieto transition into?"

"That's easy. The Crystal Bear."

"I see that you've been studying more than just a little," Tenderheart observed.

Alynia shrugged again. Studying was easy for her. The problem she had was that she wasn't very interested in lessons when she knew that she could be having adventures with her

24

feathered friends, especially Frumpy. Frumpy was always good for a laugh.

"This one's a little more difficult," Tenderheart began. "Why is the Crystal Bear constellation different from all others?"

Alynia searched her mind for the answer, stumped for a moment. Then, she remembered the answer, shouting it.

"It's the only one that crosses sky-paths with Venus!"

Tenderheart continued to quiz Alynia about the stars, because to her, nothing was more important to survival than being able to find your way at night using the stars. Alynia answered her questions, watching the Sun move across the last part of the sky.

Finally, Tenderheart asked her a final question. "Why is Venus so special?"

Alynia looked up in the sky, hoping to find the answer. She observed that the Sun was setting on the horizon and that many constellations they'd discussed were now floating in the heavens. Then, she put her finger on a thought that had been pushed to the back of her mind but that had been bothering her.

"Mother and Father are going to wake soon! I'll be in trouble if I'm out past dark!" she cried out. The thought of her father scolding her made her abandon her efforts at answering Tenderheart's final question.

Tenderheart seemed disturbed that Alynia couldn't answer her most important question, so she gave the answer to Alynia. "Venus is always locked in the Northern Sky. She will always guide you toward your destination. Most important, all constellations, except the Crystal Bear, travel around Venus, never through her. Venus becomes part of the Crystal Bear, which makes that constellation the most powerful one."

"Thanks for sharing your wisdom with me, Tenderheart," Alynia said, bowing her head. She was still thinking of how she would get home before her parents realized she'd been gone all day.

"Go ahead; climb down, dear. Head back to your village," Tenderheart said, smiling.

Alynia didn't hesitate, climbing back down through the willow's branches even more quickly than she'd climbed up. When she reached the bottom, she ran over to Frumpy, who was talking with Greyspot.

"Frumpy! We're late!" she exclaimed, scooping him up and under her arm, interrupting their conversation. Frumpy hated it when Alynia did that, for obvious reasons, especially when it was in front of other birds.

He protested until they were over a hill and out of sight, then he resigned himself to being carried back to the village, even though he wanted to finish his conversation. "You really should hear what Greyspot has to say about the Northern Woods!"

"You know how my father is!" Alynia said, a scared look in her eyes. "Especially, if I'm out after dark!"

A shiver came over Frumpy as he remembered what happened to Alynia the last time she had stayed out with the birds all day. "Maybe it will be better if I just stay at Tenderheart's willow tonight," Frumpy suggested, thinking it would be nice to wake without smelling Nabu's concoction.

"Maybe so," Alynia nodded, pausing long enough to place her friend on the path. "I'll see you as soon as I can! Make sure to tell little Poplin that I'll be back to check on him!"

Alynia then dashed faster than she had ever raced toward the river in the direction of her village. Greyspot flew past her, swooping down in front of her, and then circled back.

"Poplin and I thank you for your help when we lost our way earlier today," he said. "I'm not the spry youngling that I once was, and sometimes, I get a little lost! It was good to see you again!"

Alynia waved at him, breathless. The brush she carelessly ran through scratched her arms and legs. She didn't have the time she had taken earlier in the day to avoid all the obstacles in the woods to the west of Red Rock River. She wondered for a moment what Greyspot had meant when he'd said "again," because even though he seemed familiar to her, she was positive she'd never met him. The thought was gone as soon as she splashed into the cold waters of the river.

She emerged from the waters on the other bank soaked all the way through, clothes dripping. She tapped the gnarled trunk of the twisted tree out of habit as she passed it, resuming her quickest pace down the dirt path leading back to her village. She ran so quickly that dust came up in clouds behind her, and if Frumpy had seen her, he would have joked about how comical the dust clouds looked as they trailed off behind her feet. She made it to the border of the village just as the nightly torches were being lit.

Alynia stood behind the trees closest to a row of huts and carefully watched the movements of her fellow tribespeople. When the coast was clear, she crouched down and darted to the nearest hut. She pressed herself as closely as possible to the wall of the hut and watched as several women came around a corner to help Mother, the oldest woman in the village, as she prepared the evening's communal meal. Alynia searched the group for her mother, and when she couldn't locate her, she breathed a sigh of relief. Maybe her parents had overslept. Unfortunately, during the day, someone had put a new coat of paint on the hut, and as a result, Alynia had gotten some on her clothes. No time to worry about that, though!

At the next moment, luck was on her side. All the women were focused on their work with their backs turned to Alynia, so she sprinted into a patch of overgrown grass growing behind the next hut over. *Only one more to go*, she thought, crouching in the tall reeds. She stood to see whether she could make it to the next hut without being noticed, but to her surprise, the tribe's Mother was staring directly at her. Alynia stood, frozen in fear, but the Mother nodded and smiled at her, giving her the signal that her secret was safe. She darted from the grass to the back of her hut, pressing her ear against the wooden surface to hear if either of her parents stirred inside. She imagined that if they were, the scolding would be terrible.

27

O'stara, her mother, was always loving and understanding about Alynia's desire for adventure, but when her father Nak'te was around, her mother would stand strongly by his side. When Alynia was sure it was safe and that her parents were still asleep, she carefully tiptoed around to the front of her home. She reached inside the door and grabbed her berry basket as quietly as she could, then took off running in the direction of Sehebre's Finger.

Now, she had a story for why she was out so late because she had her basket as evidence. She just needed some berries to fill it. It made her feel proud of herself for being able to use her imagination to come up with a good excuse for why she'd been out all day. Since finding berries was one of her chores, she figured she would be in the clear. Besides, what her father didn't know wouldn't hurt him, right?

Alynia passed Nabu's hut. He was nowhere to be seen. She wondered if he was still in his sacred grounds north of the village. If so, it was a long day for him as well. Alynia took one last look around, ensuring the coast was clear. Off she went, and as always, dust clouds followed her as she made her way as quickly as she could down the path toward the berry patch.

# Chapter 3

## Crime…

"This one looks nice," Alynia said to herself as she gently picked a juicy blackberry from the bush and drew it to her lips. She closed her eyes, ready to enjoy the delicious flavors of the berry, when she heard a stern and familiar voice behind her.

"Alynia, what are you doing?"

She dropped the blackberry and turned around. Her father stood behind her in the moonlight, face illuminated by the light of a torch he carried. She had been so focused on the berry she was about to eat that she hadn't noticed him approach. He looked very angry as he stood with the torch in one hand and his other hand clenched into a fist at his hip. The torchlight cast wild shadows across his cheeks and brow as he glared at her, making him seem even more intimidating.

Nak'te stomped forward and snatched the berry basket out of Alynia's hands. He looked into it, counting the handful of berries she'd collected. In her haste to come up with a good story for why she'd been out all day, she hadn't planned an excuse for why she didn't have that many berries.

"You were out with that rooster, Frumpy, again, weren't you?" he asked.

Alynia knew that she was in trouble but still tried to get out of it. "No," she lied, her voice wavering.

"Then, how do you explain being covered in mud? What about the paint and straw all over your clothes?" Her father pointed to her clothing, trying to find a clean spot on her. "You didn't get any of that on you in the berry patch. If you've been here all day, why do you only have a handful of berries?"

Alynia looked down at herself for the first time since she'd run back to the village. It was true; she was filthy. The dust she had stirred up when she ran from the river, still wet, had clung to her clothing, creating a sticky layer of mud that had gathered in all the cracks, crevices, and folds of her outfit. Her clothes also had spots of paint from leaning against the wall of the hut. Straw from the grass she'd hidden in poked out of her pants and shirt. What a mess she was!

Anxiously, she drug her foot across the ground and kicked at some pebbles.

"I was out playing with Frumpy all day. I'm sorry I lied about it," she confessed. "I'm in a lot of trouble, aren't I?"

Nak'te set the basket down on a patch of grass. He reached his arms out to his daughter, taking her hands in his. As he knelt before her, he looked into her eyes. His expression was stern, but she thought that she could detect the faintest smirk on his face. Nak'te gave Alynia a warm, fatherly embrace, and then held her back at arm's length, examining her ruined clothing.

"Alynia, I do not punish you to hurt you. I want you to have fun and enjoy being a little girl, but you must remember that, as a tribe, we have to work together to survive. Everyone has a job to do. You must do your part!"

Alynia nodded, because she knew that she'd disappointed him, but she'd also heard this lecture from him before.

"We needed a full basket of berries for the dinner preparations tonight. Because you were out with Frumpy all day and didn't collect any, we won't have any berry pie for dessert. I'll have to apologize to the tribe Mother on your behalf," he said, scowling.

Alynia knew that fresh berry pie was one of her father's favorites, and she was a little sad because she enjoyed it as well.

"Now," commanded Nak'te, "go help your mother tend the night torches."

Alynia nodded again. Her father turned and began to make his way down the southeastern path, heading toward his nightly patrol route. She hated helping her mother with the nightly chores. When the torches went out, the smoke would get in her eyes and nose while she attempted to rekindle the flames. Her mother's chores also included collecting and organizing the hides that had been set out to tan during the day. Once they were organized, the other women of the tribe could begin to stitch them into items such as cloaks and boots. The hides were difficult to carry, and Alynia had to take special care not to drag them across the ground as she stacked them in high piles.

She walked over to the nearest berry bush, selected a juicy-looking fruit, and then carefully picked it from the branch. She drew the berry to her mouth and bit into the luscious treat, smiling as the rich flavor filled her mouth. Finally, she thought, *I get to eat dessert after all!* She really didn't want to go help her mother, regardless of her father's scolding, so she collected the basket of berries and began to make her way through the woods toward the twisted tree on the shore of Red Rock River.

"I probably shouldn't do this," she said aloud, looking to see if her father was lingering. He wasn't, though. Alynia reasoned that if she tried to help her mother in her current disheveled state, she'd end up ruining any hides she touched. So she decided to head to the river to wash off the mud and paint and shake out all the straw that had made its way into her clothes. It was getting itchy! It wouldn't take long to rinse out her shirt and pants, and it would feel good to wash the clumps of dirt out of her hair.

Following her shortcut, she continued to eat the few berries she'd managed to collect before her father surprised her. Maybe she could catch some fish at the river, which would be a better contribution to the village than a simple basket of berries, anyway. Everyone could have fresh fish for breakfast if she

31

managed to get as many as Swiftfeather had, and everyone would be so happy that they'd forgive her for not having dessert. Not only would she be able to do chores as her father had commanded her, but she'd have done extra, making him proud.

She smiled at her new plan as she reached the twisted tree. She looked around for Swiftfeather, thinking that he might be there. On nights he couldn't sleep, he sat on the shore and watched the stars, fishing and thinking about things. She scanned the shore, and then looked up into the tree branches, tapping the trunk as she always did. When she didn't see him, she walked down to the shore and began to take off her clothes.

The moonlight reflected brilliantly off the river's tranquil waters. Alynia took her time rinsing out her clothing in the cool waters, watching as the current carried the dirt and paint away. Farther out in the river, she heard fish leaping in the air, and she knew that it would be a good night for fishing. While washing her hair, she thought, *I'll catch so many fish that I'll have to get Frumpy to help me carry them home.* Then, she remembered that she'd left her spear behind and that Frumpy probably wouldn't be coming back to the village until after sunrise.

She finished washing everything off, wringing out most of the water from her clothes, then made her way back to the tree trunk. The damp clothes felt cool on her skin when she put them back on, and she sat down at the tree base for a moment to rest. It had been a long day! She'd done so much, and Frumpy had awoken her so early. Her eyelids seemed heavier than they had in as long as she could remember, and the way back to the village seemed distant.

*I'll just take a little nap*, she thought, closing her eyes. *A little nap, and then I'll go help Mother.* Before she realized it, she was asleep, snoring soundly beneath the stars and the branches of the twisted tree.

## Chapter 4

## ...and Punishment

"So," a voice boomed out of nowhere, "you like to sleep out under the stars?"

Alynia rubbed her eyes, confused. Where was she? How long had she been sleeping?

"Go ahead; wake up. You're just in time to see the sunrise." It was her father's voice.

Alynia jerked upright when she realized that she'd been asleep under the twisted tree all night. She knew there would be no getting out of the serious punishment her father would have for her this time, so she didn't say anything.

"I'm glad that you took the time to wash your hair and your clothes, Alynia," her father continued. "What do you think we should do about your blatant disregard for your responsibilities toward our village? Not sure how to answer? Don't worry, my child. I've been thinking about what we should do to teach you some responsibility—a real lesson that you won't forget or be able to get distracted from."

Her father's tone was unlike she'd ever heard it, and it made her nervous about what he would say next. She looked across the river just in time to see Frumpy return from the willow. He stopped short when he caught sight of Alynia's father

33

standing beside her, unsure of what was happening across the river.

"Come on over, rooster," Nak'te called to Frumpy, beckoning the bird to swim across and join them. "You're part of this too. If Alynia thinks you should be, that is."

"Part of... what?" Alynia timidly asked.

"Well, Alynia, the way your mother and I see it you want to roam free, spending your time away from the village, and it's obvious you're not ready for working at night with us. So, I've talked to several hunters, and they've agreed to take you along with them on their next expedition."

Frumpy made his way from the shore to the twisted tree, shaking the water out of his feathers as he walked.

"Just in time," Nak'te continued, gesturing toward the rooster. "Frumpy can go with you if you like, but I don't recommend it. The hunters are known to get hungry and rowdy, and they just might want to eat a plump rooster like you. And the predators out there wouldn't think twice about gobbling up a village bird. One bite, maybe two."

Alynia reached over to Frumpy, throwing her arms around him protectively. He didn't protest for a moment, because he knew that Nak'te was serious about what he said.

"Frumpy doesn't have to go anywhere!" Alynia declared. "He has work to do with the orphans, and he can't leave them for too long," she elaborated.

Nak'te shrugged. "Probably for the best, then. Remember what I told you last night, Alynia. Everyone has a job to do. I love you, but you don't seem to ever listen to me when I tell you nicely. I've thought about it, and I realized that maybe the jobs we're giving you aren't suitable jobs for where your interests lie. Your mother helped me come to that conclusion, because I'll admit it, I was very angry when I realized you'd come out to Red Rock River again last night."

"I'm sorry, Father," Alynia said. "I really didn't mean to fall asleep!"

34

"I know, which is why I let you sleep until dawn. You'll need the rest, child. The hunting party leaves within the hour. I'll escort you back to the village, just to make sure you don't get distracted along the way."

Alynia felt tears well in her eyes. She'd never been away for more than a night, and sometimes, hunting parties were gone for more than a week! Without Frumpy or her other feathered friends, what would she do with herself? She'd be stuck away from home with a group of seasoned hunters, men she'd never seen smile, not even when their hunts had been successful. What would Frumpy do without her to go fishing with him every day?

Frumpy nuzzled Alynia while she hugged him. "It will be fine, Alynia," he reassured her. "The hunt will go well, and you'll be back in no time!"

"But, Frumpy, I don't want to go on a hunt. The warriors are scary. They're probably all mean too!"

"They'll love you and protect you," Frumpy said.

Nak'te nodded, agreeing with him. "Are you ready to meet the hunting party, Alynia?" he asked. "It's time. You have a lot to learn."

Alynia hugged Frumpy again, squeezing him as hard as she could without crushing him. Frumpy plucked a feather from his wing and handed it to Alynia.

"For luck, and so you don't forget about me," he said.

"Take care of the birds at Tenderheart's while I'm away, especially little Poplin," she told Frumpy, placing the feather in a band around her arm. Then, she turned to her father, starting back toward the village.

"OK, Father, I'm ready to go now," she said, holding back her tears.

When they arrived at the border of the village, two men greeted them. Both men looked intimidating. The man with darker hair was muscular with a piercing gaze. He had thick

35

eyebrows and a beard that looked like dark moss. His hair was wild and untamed. The second man had lighter hair, which he wore in a ponytail tied neatly behind his head with a strip of worn leather. Several colorful feathers were woven into his hair. He was slender and looked as if he was very fast on his feet.

"So you must be our new apprentice!" the dark-haired man called out, looking at Alynia. "I'm Tun'Gusk, the leader of this hunting expedition."

"Good to see you, my friend." The slender man greeted Alynia's father, firmly shaking hands with him. Nak'te turned to Alynia and introduced her.

"This is Alynia, my daughter, and she enjoys sleeping under the stars. Perhaps so much that it may interest her to join your expedition." Alynia blushed as he pointed out her mistake from the night before to the strangers. "Alynia, as you heard, Tun'Gusk will be the leader of your party, and you are to listen to and obey him at all times. This other fellow," he paused, smiling, something that Alynia didn't see him do very often because she was always getting into trouble, "is Tapio. He's the fastest tracker in the village. Tapio will teach you better ways to race—including a lesson on how to avoid making a dust storm that covers your clothing from top to bottom."

"It is my pleasure to meet you, young Alynia. Your father told me that you're very fast on your feet. Do you think we can race some time?" Tapio asked.

Alynia liked him already. He seemed less serious than Tun'Gusk, who stood with his brow furrowed, crossed arms, and what seemed like a permanent expression of disapproval on his face.

"I love racing," she answered, becoming more interested in going on the expedition. If Tapio could teach her things about running, she'd be able to beat Frumpy, even when he tricked her into one of his head starts!

"Maybe you can show me how to run faster than ever," Tapio suggested, making Alynia blush. She hadn't expected him to be so friendly, especially suggesting that she would be able to win a race against him.

"Alynia!" her father said. "Your mother and I love you. Here is a satchel of treats for the expedition. Your mother even made a small berry pie just for you."

Alynia smiled again, stepping over to her father and wrapping her arms around him. "I'm sorry I disappointed you, Father," she apologized.

He returned her embrace for a moment, and then handed her the satchel. "Take care of yourself, and make sure you obey Tun'Gusk and Tapio, as well as the others in the hunting expedition. I will see you soon," he yawned. "As for me, it was a long night, and I have to get some sleep. Thank you for your generosity, Tun'Gusk. Look out for my daughter."

Tun'Gusk nodded. "I'll make sure that nothing eats her," he said. "We will teach her the responsibility of the hunt."

With that, her father departed, leaving Alynia with her two new friends.

"We have already packed most things we'll need on our journey," Tun'Gusk said. "Alynia, is there anything that you think we should bring along?"

Alynia thought about it for a few moments, scratching her head.

"I'm pretty good with a spear, if you think that we'll be fishing," she offered.

Tapio chuckled loudly, slapping her on the shoulder. "Little one, we'll be hunting buffalo!" he exclaimed. "A spear is a good weapon, but I'm afraid that one designed for fishing will only make a great buffalo angry!"

Alynia shrugged, unsure how to respond.

"It's a good idea, young Alynia," Tun'Gusk reassured her as they began to walk toward where the rest of the hunters were gathered. "I will see to it that an appropriate spear is included with your pack, but it will be heavy, and you will be responsible for carrying it. If you find that it is too much of a burden, I can arrange for your weapon to be a bow. Bows are good for use on

37

birds and deer, but a skilled and strong archer will be able to bring down a buffalo with only one shot."

Alynia gasped, mortified at the thought that she would have to use a bow to bring down one of her feathered friends. She didn't want to kill any living thing, but she understood that buffalo, deer, and fish were all important to her village's survival. She spoke with the birds, though; to kill one would be like killing another person, as far as she was concerned.

"I'll be fine with the spear," she answered, a chill creeping across her skin. It passed after a moment, once the bright morning sunbeams fell across her skin, warming her to the new day.

"Excellent!" declared Tun'Gusk. "We depart as soon as we are reunited with the rest of the hunters."

"It's just around the bend, there," Tapio said, nudging Alynia. "Want to race me there?"

Alynia smiled, thinking of Frumpy, and before Tapio knew it, she had taken off, gaining the advantage of a head start. She put her head down, barreling forward with all the speed she could muster, and as she approached the bend, she turned to see how far behind her Tapio was.

Tun'Gusk walked along the path at his normal brisk pace, but Tapio was nowhere to be seen. She had the passing thought that Tun'Gusk was smirking at her, but this was gone as soon as she turned her attention back to the path in front of her. She rounded the bend, but she was forced to a skidding halt by what she saw next.

Tapio stood with the rest of the hunting party, arms crossed, smiling at her. He must have noticed the look of surprise on Alynia's face as she stopped running, because he winked at her, shaking his head.

"That trick won't work on me, Alynia. I've been racing far too long!"

"How did you do that?" she asked, approaching the group.

38

"You'll learn. If you stay dedicated to the hunt and follow orders, you'll be amazed at the useful things you can learn."

Still confused about how he managed to get to the party so quickly, Alynia reached out and poked Tapio in the arm, making sure that he was real and that it wasn't some trick. He laughed again.

"I'm no illusion," he said, adjusting his ponytail. Alynia looked at the feathers in his hair and then touched the feather that Frumpy had given her earlier that morning. She missed him already.

Tun'Gusk arrived a moment later, greeting the other hunters. There were nine people in the party, including Alynia, Tun'Gusk, and Tapio. Tun'Gusk introduced Alynia to the other six hunters.

"This is Alynia, and this will be her first hunt. She is here as a favor to her father, because she isn't one for following through with responsibilities."

Alynia blushed again, wondering how often her mistake from the day before would be mentioned.

"As such," Tun'Gusk continued, "I expect you all to guide her in the ways of the hunt, teach her new skills, protect her from danger, and be as stern as necessary if she begins to stray from the path because of petty distractions."

Tun'Gusk might be sterner than her father was, Alynia thought, worried that he would be angry with her for any mistakes she might make in the coming days. The other hunters nodded in acknowledgment of Tun'Gusk.

"We are going to head east for this hunt, passing Sehebre's Finger, and making for the rolling hills and grassy plains in search of buffalo. If we bring home enough buffalo, our stores will be replenished, and there will be a great feast upon our return," he explained.

The hunters cheered at the suggestion of the feast. Alynia looked them over as they began to pack their gear. There were four men and two women hunters, and they all looked

39

serious to Alynia. She noticed that they all were extremely fit physically; she concluded that they were all seasoned hunters who had been on many expeditions.

One man was dressed in strange clothing that incorporated vines and leaves. She suspected his unusual outfit would help him sneak up on his prey. Another man smoked a pipe, and Alynia watched as he puffed, blowing rings of smoke in the air. He had a closely cut beard that matched his bright, orange hair. He had a quiver of arrows slung across his back, and a massive longbow leaned against a large stone beside him.

The other two men were twin brothers. Alynia could tell because they looked exactly alike. These men carried spears, but on their hips, they wore holsters holding something she had only seen a few times before—slingshots! She'd always wanted to try using one. Maybe the men would let her try them out sometime, she thought.

Alynia noted the two women in the party. They were both very beautiful to her. The first woman had dark skin, and her hair was black, except one gray streak that ran through her hair on the right side of her head. The woman's clothes were also made of black leather and lined with fur, and Alynia thought that it would probably be too warm in the afternoons for the woman to keep wearing such thick clothing.

The second woman was especially interesting to her. She had several strings of beads woven into her thick, matted hair and many scars on her arms and legs, as if she had seen many battles in her life. A long, thick scar ran horizontally across the woman's face, passing right over her cheeks and nose. Alynia approached her, holding out her hand for the woman to shake it. She looked at Alynia's hand, then at Alynia's face distastefully.

"I like your hair," Alynia began. "It's..."

"Listen, kid," the woman interrupted, "I don't want to babysit you on this expedition, but if Tun'Gusk orders it, I'll do so. Try not to get in my way."

Alynia was taken aback by the woman's shortness with her. She missed her friends; they would never speak to her like that.

"Nothing personal," the woman added, almost as an afterthought.

Alynia walked over to Tapio, who held her pack for her, waiting.

"Don't mind her," Tapio said. "Her name's Nakono, and she takes hunting very seriously. She's a great gal once you get to know her!"

"How did she get those scars?" Alynia asked.

"That's a story for her to tell you," Tapio replied, handing Alynia her pack with a heavy spear.

Alynia lifted the spear as high as she could over her head, testing its weight. She tossed it in her hands, spinning it in half-circles, and then examined the sharpened tip, which looked like it could slice even the thickest leather. The spear's blunt end was capped with a bronze sheath dented and tarnished with age.

"This spear belonged to an old hunter who is no longer with us named Ohtas. It is a great responsibility to carry it," Tapio explained. "You should take note of the notches carved into the hilt. Those are marks for each kill made with the spear. Perhaps you'll be adding your own notches by the end of this expedition. The other hunters believe that this spear is filled with good luck. Now, I must go and ensure that the rest of the party is prepared for the journey. Make sure that your pack is tightly bound. If you lose your bedding, no one will share their blanket with you, and sometimes, it gets cold at night!" He then made his way to the other hunters, leaving Alynia with her new weapon.

She made a few practice jabs with the spear, and then tossed it as hard as she could toward a nearby tree. It fell disappointingly short of her target. She wasn't used to the weight of the spear, as it was easily twice the size of the fishing spear she'd been borrowing from her father. It would take some practice, she thought, picking it off the ground. She turned and noticed Tun'Gusk watching her. His expression was blank. She

41

wondered what he was thinking about her and whether he was judging her harshly.

A few minutes later, all the hunters were prepared, so the party started making its way east toward Sehebre's Finger.

## Chapter 5

## On the Hunt

On the morning of the third day of the hunt, Alynia awoke to the escalating voices of her fellow hunters arguing about the next direction they should go while searching for buffalo. She opened her eyes, rolling over on her sleeping mat, while slowly pulling her blanket away from her face. Tun'Gusk was nowhere to be seen. Tapio still seemed asleep, though Alynia couldn't see how anyone could sleep through the hunters' morning banter. She'd learned their names over the past few days, because hunting had been unfruitful, and she was too nervous about Tun'Gusk to venture away from the party for long. She stretched, listening to what they were saying.

"I haven't seen a single print of the herd since we embarked," the woman known as Kauket said. She had her black hair tied up in two buns today, highlighting the silver streak on the right side of her hair in the morning light. Even though she seemed angry, she still looked very pretty to Alynia.

"Just because you haven't seen them doesn't mean they're not there," Segomo, the party's other tracker, argued. He had recently added some fresh stems of grass to his wardrobe, reminding Alynia of how she'd looked on the night she'd crept back from Tenderheart's far too late. "They're farther to the east. They must have migrated farther away this season in search of better grazing."

Alynia looked into the clouds above, admiring the way the morning light was causing them to turn from shades of pink into bright white puffs, drifting slowly above her.

"I don't think Tun'Gusk knows where the herd is going this time," Kauket muttered.

One of the twin brothers, Tomas, spoke up. Alynia sat up to listen to what he said. "My brother Paulo and I have been on many expeditions that began without much luck. Once, I came close to giving up on hunting altogether. We had been camping in the wilderness for weeks, and there wasn't a single sign of game in the area. Our village was expecting us to return with much needed game, and our supplies for the hunt had been exhausted. Paulo continued to believe in Tun'Gusk's ability to lead us, although my doubts had gotten the best of me. In time, we had one of our best hunts ever."

"That was a long time ago, Tomas," Nakono said as she sharpened one of her many blades. The sound of her whetstone scraping across the metal was rhythmic and controlled. She sharpened the edge of the weapon without even focusing on her movements, trained and practiced as she was with her blade.

"What I'm saying is that even though things seem hopeless at times, if we just have faith, they will work out in the end," Tomas explained.

"Usually!" Paulo laughed, poking at the fire with a stick.

Lurs sat quietly smoking his pipe, watching the others. Alynia rolled up her bedding and then made her way over to sit beside him. She liked the way his pipe smelled, and he didn't mind when she stood near him or sat beside him. He nodded at her and broke off a piece of his morning bread ration for her when she sat. She reached into her pack and pulled out a small green apple, handing it to him. He accepted her gift, still silent, placing it in the pocket of his vest.

Tun'Gusk arrived at the camp, appearing from nowhere. He kicked at Tapio as he passed, waking the still sleeping man.

"Get up, Tapio, we're waiting on you," he said. "So what's everyone discussing this morning?"

44

Alynia looked at everyone, unsure of what would happen next. None of the hunters answered Tun'Gusk as he stood in front of them, tapping his foot on the ground impatiently. He stretched his muscular arms, yawning.

"Alynia!" he declared, turning his attention toward her. "What were they talking about? Something about how I don't know how to hunt, I presume." With this, he laughed.

"Well, sir, they were just saying that, sometimes, things aren't what they seem," she said, hoping that she wouldn't get anyone in trouble. Nakono glared at her from across the camp.

"Please explain, little one," Tun'Gusk requested.

"It's just that we want to have the hunt go well from the start," she explained. "And it doesn't always happen like we want it to. But in the end, the hunt usually yields something for the tribe, even if it takes longer than we expect it to."

"Very good, Alynia," Tun'Gusk said. "It's best for you to remember that. All of you! Believe it or not, I do know what I'm doing. Alynia, most of these hunters have been on countless expeditions with me. They're just bickering with each other for the entertainment of it, really. If they didn't enjoy the pursuit, none of them would be here."

Alynia cautiously smiled. Tun'Gusk seemed to be finally warming up to her. If only Nakono would do the same!

Tapio came over to Alynia, shaking the sleep off his arms and legs as he walked.

"What do you say we have a race today?" he asked her, holding out his hand to help her up from the ground.

"I'd love it!" she exclaimed, eager to do something besides carry her pack behind the rest of the hunters. "But where will we race to?"

"How about to that rock formation on the hill over there?" Tapio pointed to a pile of rocks a fair distance from the camp. "It's a long race, though. Do you think you will be able to make it?"

45

The other hunters had risen to observe the race, forming a half-circle around Tapio and Alynia.

"I can make it. Just tell me when you're ready," she said, stretching her legs.

"You're not going to try to cheat and get a head start this time?" Tapio asked with a raised eyebrow, tilting his head a little to the side.

"Will it do any good?" Alynia answered, hoping that this would be her chance to discover his secret way of winning the last race.

"OK, Lurs, if you'd be so kind as to count down for us..."

Lurs nodded, gesturing a countdown with his hand, never removing the pipe from his mouth. Three fingers. Two fingers. One. Then they were both off, running as quickly as they could toward the distant rocks.

Alynia put all her energy into her legs, willing her feet to go faster, but Tapio stayed beside her, effortlessly keeping pace with her. He smiled at her.

"Try harder," he said, moving a few paces ahead.

She could feel the sweat breaking across her brow. She concentrated on the ground beneath her, kicking up dust as she always did. She noticed that Tapio wasn't making dirt fly into the air. He seemed as cool and calm as ever.

"How is this so easy for you?" Alynia asked, falling a few more paces behind him.

"Your feet are heavy, Alynia. You push them as hard as you can into the ground, and you don't focus on the distant rocks. You only see the step in front of you."

"I don't want to trip and fall," she explained, out of breath.

"You won't trip and fall if you trust yourself. You know what the path to the rocks ahead looks like, don't you? Haven't you already envisioned the progress of the race in your mind's eye?"

It was true. She'd imagined that she could win the race against Tapio, but that wasn't turning out to be the case. He was getting farther and farther ahead of her with each of his strides, and she was running out of her initial burst of racing speed more quickly than she thought she would.

"Close your eyes for a moment," he continued. "You won't fall."

She closed her eyes, listening to him as she ran.

"See the path as it is in your memory. Focus on the details of each coming step while paying careful attention to the rocks ahead. They are your goal, so do not be afraid to make great strides to get to them," he said.

Her eyes were still closed, but she found that the physical act of running was occupying less of her attention than it had just a moment before.

"Now, open your eyes," he said.

She opened her eyes and discovered that she had gained some of the distance back that he had put between them. They were already halfway to the rocks. Maybe she would beat him after all!

"See what I mean?" Tapio asked, and then accelerated faster than she thought was possible. He doubled the distance between them in a few long steps. She was discouraged by this development, but she didn't stop running. Everyone was watching from the camp. She didn't want to look as if she'd given up only halfway through the race.

"This is impossible!" she protested, panting.

"Nothing is impossible," he replied. "The earth below your feet is also your mother. A mother to us all. Tread lightly. Like I said, your feet are heavy, and you're pushing them down into the ground as hard as you can. There is too much resistance in your motion this way. Move through the distance. Imagine yourself like a bird, if it helps."

She realized that he was right. She was pushing downward with as much force as possible, which was why she kicked up so much dirt every time she ran.

"Focus on the rocks, Alynia. Put your energy into running forward, not downward! Fly with your feet!" Tapio called to her, rapidly approaching their goal.

She closed her eyes again, envisioning the rocks, traveling along the path of the race in her mind while shifting the way she directed her motion. Running seemed easier when she did this; she opened her eyes again, surprised that it was starting to work. She was kicking up less dust and now gaining on Tapio.

He reached the rocks before her, though, leaning against them while he waited for her to catch up. She could hear the other hunters cheering in the distance when he finished the race, but she was surprised to hear them continue even after he stopped running.

"They're cheering for you, Alynia," he yelled. "They might act tough and mean, but they love a good race, and this was a close one!"

It didn't feel like a very close race. Tapio had beaten her by almost a minute. She'd made it to the rocks in record time, but it still wasn't as fast as Tapio. She leaned against the rocks with him, catching her breath, and shaking some remaining dust from her shirt and pants.

"You did an excellent job," he said, putting his hand on her shoulder. "You understood what I was teaching you much faster than I thought you would. You show a lot of potential, little one!"

"I'll keep trying," Alynia responded. "If anything, that will help me win races against most birds. I like what you said about flying, Tapio."

"I thought that you would. Your father told me that you really enjoy spending time with birds out at Red Rock River. I've known your father for years, and he comes across as harsh sometimes, but he really just wants the best for you."

"I know. I always let him down, though, don't I?" Alynia asked, remembering her mistakes.

"I don't think you've ever *really* let him down," Tapio said. "I think that he just wants you to understand that life isn't all about games and playing all day. Sometimes, he forgets what it's like to be a kid, though. That's all." Tapio put his arm around Alynia's shoulder, hugging her, because he could see that she was getting sad thinking about her father.

"Thanks, Tapio," Alynia said, determined not to cry over it. "You're really nice. You're like a cool big brother."

Tapio smiled, pleased at her comment. "Alynia, I was just thinking the same thing about you. You're like the fast little sister I always wanted but never had! I'll teach you to race faster than anyone else in the village, just as I would have if I had a sister!"

They sat for a moment longer and then it was time to return to the camp. Everyone was probably packed and ready to continue onward in search of the buffalo herd.

"Race back?" Alynia asked, and Tapio laughed.

"OK," he said, already running toward the rest of the hunters.

"No fair!" Alynia cried out.

"Why not? You did it to me the first time we raced!"

She shook her head, running behind him as fast as she could, focusing on the techniques he'd taught her. By the time they reached the group, she'd almost caught up to him.

"I would have won if you didn't get a head start," she said between breaths. She wiped the sweat from her forehead.

"You might have tied me," he conceded, "but you're not fast enough yet to win!"

She picked up her things and began to follow the others, snacking on one of her green apples. As she crunched the tart fruit, she thought about racing and whether she could beat Tapio in a race before the hunt was over. Her legs ached a little from the exercise of the past few days, especially after she'd run such a long distance so quickly so early in the morning. *I'll beat him*, she thought. *I'll find a way!* She threw the apple core to a groundhog she saw peeking up from its little house in the field they were passing and reached for another in her pack. She was glad to be on this journey, though they hadn't encountered any buffalo.

—

## Chapter 6

## A Sign From Above

Several days passed, and the party continued to search for buffalo without luck. Both Kauket and Segomo agreed that the herd had migrated beyond the village's normal hunting range and recommended that the expedition return to the village empty-handed to wait until later in the season for the herd to return to the area.

The hunters engaged in idle talk among themselves about the old legends, imagining what the ancient ones must have been like, but Alynia was bored with their conversations because they never included her. Tun'Gusk had grown exceptionally foul, his disappointment with the hunt beginning to show on his face. As for Tapio, he had scouted ahead of the group every day with Kauket and Segomo, running messages between the main group and the trackers about their lack of findings regarding the buffalo herd. Due to his absence, Alynia hadn't been able to race him again.

None of them wanted to go back to the village empty-handed, because they all looked forward to the prospect of having a victorious feast upon their return. They could imagine the fresh buffalo steaks, delicious breads and fruits, dancing, singing, and storytelling that would come with a return feast; it would be unfortunate if they missed such a celebration. Therefore, they continued their trek eastward.

51

Alynia wanted to return to the village, though, because her birthday was coming up, and she didn't want to be away from the village and her friends, the birds, when it happened.

"I'll never get home from this stupid expedition," she said to herself, slowly drifting away from the group. She gazed across the long fields around them, watching the grass sway in the wind. She stared up at the clouds, imagining the faces of Frumpy, Poplin, and Swiftfeather in their billowing shapes. She imagined buffalo in the clouds, and then pretended to throw her spear as high as she could into the air, taking the biggest one down, enabling her to return home in time for her birthday.

She thought that she was imagining it when she saw the shape of a bird flying in circles overhead, but after further inspection, she realized that it was a falcon of some sort. It was too high for her to distinguish any of its markings, but she was sure that they were too far from home for her to know who the bird was. She remembered what Tapio said about pretending to be a bird when she ran, so she decided to practice running. She started running in wide circles, mimicking the path of the bird so high in the air above her, arms stretched at her sides.

She continued to copy the bird's path, running faster and faster, imagining that she was with the bird in the clouds, looking down on the hunters as they moved through the plains. After a while, she called to the falcon. "Come down; come down. Tell me your name!" The bird began to descend in slow arcs toward Alynia.

Tun'Gusk noticed that she had strayed a significant distance from the rest of the group and started making his way toward her, instructing the rest of the party to continue east while he went to fetch her. He heard her making noises while looking at the sky, but he couldn't make out what she was saying. He looked up, noticing the falcon's descent. *Interesting*, he thought. *I wonder how she always finds a bird to befriend.*

The falcon landed on the ground near Alynia once she stopped running in circles.
"Why are you copying my flight with your dance, young human?" the falcon asked. Her feathers were dark, almost black, and her eyes were a golden yellow. Alynia had never seen a

falcon with these colors.

"Your flight is amazing and beautiful," Alynia answered. "I wish that I could fly like you."

"You are kind, human. What is your name?"

"My name's Alynia. What's yours?"

"My name is Moonshade. I am from a land far to the south and east of here, and I am making a pilgrimage so I may better understand the world we live in. What is the purpose of your journey? I haven't seen any human villages for days, so you must be on a quest yourself. Am I correct?"

"My companions and I are searching for buffalo for a hunting expedition," Alynia explained. "But we're not having very much luck. It seems that the herds have moved farther away from our village than they normally do. It's pretty boring out here, if you ask me." She kicked at a pebble on the ground.

"What would you rather be doing?" Moonshade asked.

"I'd rather be spending time with my other friends who are also birds!" Alynia exclaimed, fondly remembering her companions back home.

"I noticed that you speak quite well," Moonshade said, then turned her attention toward Tun'Gusk, who was getting closer to them. "Who is the big man coming our way?"

Alynia turned and looked at Tun'Gusk, who had slowed his advance when he realized that they were talking about him.

"That's Tun'Gusk. He's the leader of our party. He looks scary, but I think beneath the surface, he's a wise and skillful hunter who means you no harm."

Alynia, who sounded as if she were squawking and cooing like the bird she was obviously speaking to, baffled Tun'Gusk. He didn't realize that she could *actually* talk to birds and had assumed that she was only pretending to do so, that her stories were just figments of a playful child's overactive imagination.

"Are you *actually* speaking to that bird, Alynia?" Tun'Gusk asked, seeking verification of his suspicion.

"Of course, I am!" she answered, rolling her eyes. "Her name's Moonshade, by the way."

"If it's buffalo you seek, you're heading in the wrong direction," Moonshade advised Alynia. "You need to head south for another day or two. That's where the closest herd has roamed to."

Alynia conveyed this information to Tun'Gusk, who wasn't sure whether she was making it up or whether the bird was telling the truth. He still felt surprised that the rumors about Alynia speaking to birds were true.

"There's never been a herd spotted so far south," Tun'Gusk said. "We will discuss it with the others. Please tell Moonshade that I am grateful for the advice." He bowed slightly and then started walking toward the rest of the group.

"Would you like to join us? You can be a scout for our party. Because you can go so high, you'll be able to see where we need to go!" Alynia was excited at the idea of having a bird as a companion for part of the trip. She thought that they should have brought Frumpy along. They hadn't encountered any danger since they'd departed, and he would have been great at keeping up everyone's spirits.

Moonshade considered it for just a moment and then agreed to accompany Alynia and the hunters. She took off into the air, flying in quick, darting arcs around Alynia who began to dance with joy. *Finally!* Alynia thought. Finally, someone she could talk to on this journey.

When they rejoined the rest of the hunters, Tun'Gusk suggested that they take Moonshade's advice and head south in search of the herd. The hunters were open to the idea because they hadn't had any luck on their current route. They trusted the bird's unique perspective as a scout and that her advice was sound, welcoming her to the party, which made Alynia even happier. The hunters raised their eyebrows, thinking about how strange it was that the little girl was speaking in the language of the birds and leading them in a new direction. Even Nakono pushed her doubts about Alynia's credibility as a member of the group to the side once they started moving south.

After a few hours, Tun'Gusk stopped the party for a light meal at the base of a grassy ridge. Moonshade had been sitting on Alynia's shoulder for a while, talking about the land she had come from, as Alynia listened intently to her tales of places far away. As the hunters broke bread together, Tapio and Kauket went ahead to scout for signs of the buffalo herd because they'd recently spotted tracks in the dust.

Tomas and Paulo had been gathering pebbles as they marched southward. They gathered their pebbles into one pile as they ate, happy with their collection. Then they took turns choosing the best ones from the pile, two at a time.

"What are you doing?" Alynia asked, turning her head sideways. Sometimes, she moved like the birds she had been talking to, especially when she'd been speaking to them for a long period.

"It's a game we invented while hunting years ago," Paulo explained. "We take turns selecting the best stones of the bunch, and then we use our slingshots to try to strike distant targets. Whoever hits the mark first gets a point, and after you get enough points, you win a prize—usually it's Tomas' lunch!" he laughed.

"He exaggerates," Tomas disagreed. "He only wins every now and then. Usually, it's his lunch in my belly. And his dinner!"

"How do you know what the best rocks are?" Alynia asked.

"You have to select the ones smooth enough to slice the air and with just the right balance of weight to soar the distance required," Tomas answered. "If your stones are too heavy, they will fall to the earth far too early. If they are too rough, they will veer off the course. If you choose stones that are too light, they could do anything, but they will definitely go too far."

"One time, I shot a stone that was so smooth and so light that it is probably still flying in the air!" Paulo boasted, causing the other hunters to shake their heads.

Segomo stopped gathering bundles of grass for his camouflage for a moment, selecting a long and slender reed from his collection. He threw the reed at Paulo like an arrow, and it struck Paulo in the arm.

"Hey!" cried Paulo, protesting.

"I once fired an arrow that did the same thing," Segomo said.

"I once threw an axe into the sky, and it went so high that it still has not landed," added Tun'Gusk. "I miss that axe. I wonder if it is on the Moon."

Alynia loved that everyone was joking around and telling stories. Their moods had improved dramatically since they'd met Moonshade and started in the new direction. Alynia considered Moonshade good luck.

"I'm glad you're with us," she whispered to the bird.

"I'm glad you're letting me come along," chuckled Moonshade.

Just then, Tapio came running over the ridge as fast as he could. "Buffalo are just over the ridge!" he exclaimed, more excited than Alynia had ever seen. "Kauket is watching the herd in case they start to migrate, but we should be able to take them by early evening!"

"Excellent work, Tapio!" Tun'Gusk smiled. "Moonshade, would you be so kind as to verify the size of the herd for us?"

The falcon took off into the air without saying a word and soared over the ridge. It wasn't long before she became the tiniest black dot in the bright-blue sky, so small that Alynia could barely see her. The other hunters began to unpack their gear, making a base camp where they had sat. Lurs, to Alynia's surprise, extinguished his pipe and placed it in a leather pouch on his side. He began to stretch his arms and his legs, then tested the strength of his bow by pulling back the bowstring several times in rapid succession.

Moonshade returned and confirmed the news that the herd was nearby. "There are at least one hundred buffalo in the herd," she announced, landing next to Tun'Gusk. "You'll have to be careful not to send them running over the ridge in this direction, or they might trample you!"

"We will plan ahead, Moonshade," Tun'Gusk said. "Were there any notable features of the land that might be of use to us?"

"I did take note of a series of small hills farther to the south, just past where the herd is currently grazing. There are some trees that might be useful as a hiding spot on the hills."

"The herd might choose to seek shade from the late afternoon sun beneath the trees," Segomo advised. "I've seen it happen often before. They might spend the night there, but if we make it to the trees before dusk, we should be able to surprise them."

"That's an excellent idea," Tun'Gusk said. "However, some of us should stay here at the camp in the event the herd comes this way. Our strongest warriors should remain. Paulo and Tomas, you are an excellent team, and your marksmanship with both your slings and your spears is unparalleled. You should stay here."

The twins nodded, agreeing with Tun'Gusk. They reached for their spears, examining them to ensure that they were ready for use in the hunt.

"Tapio and Alynia, you are our best runners," Tun'Gusk continued. "You should make your way around the herd as quickly as possible, then over to the hills and behind the trees. The rest of us will covertly cross the ridge to rejoin Kauket, where we will continue our advance. Moonshade will signal you when we are prepared to begin, and then you will come out from the trees, running toward the herd as fast as you can, scaring them and sending them right toward us!"

It was more responsibility than Alynia knew what to do with! She blushed at the compliment Tun'Gusk had given her about her running ability, though she knew in her heart that it was the truth. She was a very fast runner. It made her proud that she'd learned to race and had improved her skill by following Tapio's advice.

"Right," Tapio said. "Alynia is a good choice. Are you ready to set our trap, little one?"

"I'm ready!" Alynia exclaimed, trying to sound as bold as possible.

"We should go now. I hope your snack was enough to tide you over until tonight when we will feast on buffalo," Tapio laughed, patting his belly comically.

"Before you go," Nakono said, approaching Alynia, "I want you to take this. It is for good luck, which you will need, because this is your first hunt, and you have a daunting task ahead of you. Spooking a herd of buffalo is a dangerous thing. This token will help keep you safe and brave." She handed a smoothly polished ruby gemstone to Alynia. It looked as if it had been worn away by years of handling, but even then, it still shone as bright as fire. It had a magical quality to it, Alynia thought, as she admired how it sparkled in the sunlight.

"It's so pretty! Where did you get it?" Alynia asked.

"I acquired it on a journey through the Land Lit by Fire," Nakono said.

"Thank you, Nakono," Alynia said, surprised by Nakono's kind gesture. She placed the gem in her pouch.

"It's not much, but it will help you when you need it. When you first joined our group, I thought you would be a burden. Now, I believe that you will prove me wrong," Nakono said. "Now, go!"

Tapio began to run along the ridge, heading in the direction of the stand of trees Moonshade had described. Alynia followed as quickly as she could, trying to keep up, and for the most part, keeping up with him.

Live free
Dream loud
Be inspired
Find your power

## Chapter 7

## Did You See That?

When the group arrived at the trees, they rested long enough to catch their breath, looking back across the plains at the grazing herd between them and the rest of their friends. Tapio pointed out where Tun'Gusk hid in the tall grass. Alynia could only see him because he was so massive that it was difficult for him to hide completely. She couldn't see Segomo because he was camouflaged by the grasses he'd collected. Tapio pointed out that the buffalo hadn't noticed that the hunters were near, and the wind had been favorable because their scent had remained undetected as well. If the buffalo smelled or saw the hunters before everyone was in position, they might panic and run in every direction, making it much more difficult to take down any of them.

"The past few days all come together at this point," Tapio said, gesturing toward the earth with his hands. "We are going to run toward the herd as quickly as we can. You can scream at them if you want to. Our job is to cause them to bolt in the direction of Tun'Gusk and the others so they can pounce on several buffalo at once, making our hunt the most successful."

"Is it OK that I'm nervous? I feel as though a flock of sparrows is in my stomach, trying to get out of my throat!" Alynia said, causing Tapio to chuckle.

60

"Of course, it's OK to be nervous. I'm nervous. I'm sure that Tun'Gusk and all the others are nervous too. It's just that we've learned that you don't have to let your nervousness stop you from achieving your goal." He patted her on the shoulder. "You'll see, soon enough. It's not nearly as bad as you imagine it will be. It never is! Are you ready? I can see Moonshade now."

Alynia looked up into the sky, locating Moonshade quickly. She turned her head slightly so she could hear better, waiting for Moonshade's piercing call. The shriek would signal that it was time for them to advance. It was like a game, Alynia thought, like a race of sorts. Who better to race beside than Tapio?

Then, she heard it, coming down from above like an arrow. "Go! Hurry!" screamed Moonshade, and Alynia bolted from her hiding place behind the trees, temporarily leaving Tapio. She ran with all her might, flailing her arms in a way she thought would make her seem bigger and scarier to the buffalo. A few buffalo spotted her and began to run away, heading toward the rest of the hunters, just as Tun'Gusk had planned.

Tapio joined Alynia in making noise, his whooping voice booming across the field, startling the rest of the herd into motion. A sound like thunder rose from the prairie as the buffalo stampeded toward the hidden hunters, and dust rose from the ground in mighty clouds. The herd moved like the waters of a river around stones, moving away from Alynia and Tapio, instinctively sheltering the smallest calves in the center of the group. These calves were too small to be hunted, anyway, but the buffalo didn't know that.

Alynia continued her advance, moving in a slightly different direction from Tapio, because she'd seen that some of the herd was turning and doubling back, and she didn't want any of the best ones to get away. The dust clouds moved toward her, riding a sudden breeze, and just before her vision of the far ridge was obscured, she saw Tun'Gusk and the rest of the hunters rise out of the waving grasses, weapons readied. They seemed larger than life in that split second, but she couldn't concentrate on them for long. She knew that she had to keep her mind on the immediate task of frightening the herd toward the ridge, so she doubled her cries, leaping through the air as she ran.

Suddenly, out of the dust, a shape caught her attention. It looked like a buffalo, but as she squinted her eyes, she couldn't be sure. The noise of hundreds of hooves pounding the earth filled her ears. She could feel her heart beating in her ears above that. Sweat had starting dripping from her forehead into her eyes.

*What is that?* she wondered, slowing, and then stopping in her tracks. It definitely looked like a buffalo, except it seemed ghostly white, and it was walking directly toward her, unlike the rest of the stampeding beasts.

Another gust of wind came, clearing the dust from the air around Alynia. She could clearly see the animal now. She was correct—a white buffalo calf had emerged from the herd, and it looked right at her as it walked toward her. The buffalo's beauty mesmerized Alynia, compelling her to walk toward it. All the rest of the noise and activity began to diminish around her. A moment later, her focus fixed on the animal approaching her, all she could hear was the sound of her breathing and heartbeat.

She was now almost within arm's length of the beautiful buffalo calf, which had an aura glowing around it. She stared into its dark eyes, which seemed as black as the darkest moonless night. Though dark, its eyes sparkled as if they were filled with bands of stars. The ghostly calf stared back at Alynia, continuing its advance toward her. She reached out her hand to touch it, slowly closing the few remaining steps between them. The buffalo lowered its head, ready for her to touch it right between its ears.

Without warning, Alynia felt a rough blow to her side, jarring her senses back in full force. The air knocked out of her, she struggled to breathe and hit the ground, scraping her shoulder in the fall. The grit of the rocky soil dug into her skin, burning it. Although she wanted to keep staring at the mesmerizing white buffalo, she had to close her eyes, forcing back tears. She felt a weight on top of her that she tried to resist, but she couldn't break free.

"Stop fighting me! Stop moving!" a familiar voice shouted, close to her ear. The sound of the herd had magnified tenfold, and Alynia realized that they must have doubled back on themselves, changing their course to lead them to the stand of trees instead.

"Tapio?" Alynia asked, still clenching her eyes shut. It sounded as if the angry hooves of buffalo were stampeding right next to her head.

"Be still!" Tapio loudly answered, his voice hoarse from rousing the buffalo. "The herd's almost passed us!"

Alynia waited for what seemed like an eternity, trying not to squirm too much in anticipation of a buffalo's angry, stomping foot crashing down on her. She thought about what she'd seen before Tapio had tackled her. She'd never heard of a white buffalo before. She wondered what made it special and different. She couldn't wait to tell Frumpy and Poplin about it, that is, if she made it through the stampede in one piece!

Eventually, the sound of the trampling herd diminished, and she felt Tapio roll off her. He had protected her from the herd's charge by curling over her so that the buffalo would move around them.

"Are you OK, Alynia?" Tapio asked, checking her for bruises and cuts. He frowned when he saw that her shoulder had been scraped in the fall.

"Why did you knock me to the ground?" Alynia asked. "I was just about to touch the white buffalo, but you stopped me. Is it dangerous?"

"White buffalo? I never saw a white buffalo. Just you, standing there as if in a trance, about to get mauled by one of the biggest bulls I've ever seen."

"It was right there!" Alynia insisted, gesturing toward the spot that she'd last seen the buffalo coming from. "It was walking right toward me, quite peacefully. It was a beautiful calf with eyes like night. Have you ever seen anything like that before?"

Tapio scowled, taking Alynia's head in his hands, gently inspecting it for bruises.

63

"Little sister, are you sure that you weren't stomped in the head? Did you hit your head on the ground when I knocked you down?" He had a very concerned look on his face as he held up three fingers in front of Alynia. "How many fingers am I holding up?"

"Six!" joked Alynia, laughing, as Tapio's eyes grew wide. "I'm joking. My head feels fine, Tapio."

He still seemed worried, patting the dirt from their clothes. Tun'Gusk, Nakono, and Lurs approached a moment later.

"Paulo and Tomas came over the ridge when they heard the stampede," Tun'Gusk said. "A good thing, too, because they were able to make an additional kill before the herd changed direction."

"Lurs and I bagged a second beast, one of the largest," Nakono said. Lurs nodded in approval, reaching for his pipe.

"Segomo and Kauket took down another, and they are dressing the animals now," Tun'Gusk continued. "This was a moderately successful hunt, though we could have used the meat and hide from another buffalo. However, there will be plenty to eat tonight, and it will be plenty of work to haul the rest back to the village in time for the Feast of Returning."

Alynia looked at Tapio who made his way over to Tun'Gusk and whispered something in his ear. She couldn't make out what Tapio said, but whatever it was, it changed Tun'Gusk's demeanor immediately. He stared at Alynia with his penetrating gaze, mysterious and unreadable. She gulped, nervous for a different reason than earlier. She hoped that she hadn't ruined their part of the hunt and that the other hunters wouldn't blame her for not capturing a fourth animal.

Moonshade descended from the sky, perching on Alynia's shoulder. "I'm glad that's over. The dust storm that herd kicked up was tremendous!" she said, stretching one of her wide, black wings. Knowing that the hunters didn't understand her language, she continued to speak to Alynia.

"What happened? Why did you stop running?"

64

"I saw something," Alynia explained, "but Tapio said it wasn't there. Did you see what I was looking at?"

Moonshade blinked, remembering. "You stopped running and then stood still for a long moment, then began walking toward the center of the herd, toward where the youngest buffalo were sheltered. This angered the bigger buffalo who changed direction and charged you. The rest of the herd followed. What did you see?"

"I saw a white buffalo. I've never seen anything like it."

"If you believe that you saw it, though I did not, and Tapio did not, then I believe you," Moonshade said. "You know what you saw more than any of us. Your sight is your own; your vision is your gift. Falcons like me, we have learned from the time we are hatchlings to rely on our sight, as well as trust the sight of others in our flock."

Alynia smiled at Moonshade's implication. "We're your flock now?" she asked.

"As I am part of yours," answered Moonshade, playfully nipping at a strand of Alynia's hair.

They all began to walk back to the camp, congratulating one another, singing songs of a victorious hunt. Alynia listened as they chanted:

*Through ancient times to modern days,*

*Sehebre's finger points the way.*

*Successful hunt was to be found*

*The drifting herd, hunters surround*

*Through smarts and toil, we captured food,*

*But don't forget this interlude:*

*Give thanks to all beasts we've caught*

*Give thanks, we always, as we ought*

65

*A promised hunt, successful hunt*

*Yeah, hey ho! Yeah, hey ho!*

She'd never seen them all so happy in the whole journey, and it reminded her that her birthday was coming. She hoped that they all would be there. Their camaraderie made her miss her bird friends more than ever, especially Frumpy. At least she'd be back home in a few days, and then she could see them again.

She wondered what Poplin was doing at Tenderheart's and if he was adjusting well to his new home. She wondered how many fish Swiftfeather had been catching in the mornings and whether he had been sleeping better.

As they moved back across the plains, she looked behind them and saw the rest of the buffalo herd moving away in the distance. She tried to see the white buffalo calf again, but she didn't have any luck. Once they were back at their camp and had prepared the buffalo for transport back to the village, they made a huge bonfire on which they began to roast tremendous buffalo steaks, one for each and two for Tun'Gusk whose stomach was growling almost as loud as thunder.

As they finished their meal, the hunters recounted the events of the day, boasting about their contribution to the hunt. Each took a turn exaggerating his importance in the expedition's success. When it came to Alynia's turn, she sat silently, still worried that Tun'Gusk or Tapio would blame her for almost being trampled.

"Why are you so quiet, little girl?" joked Tomas.

"She's still out of breath from having to run, I'm sure!" Tapio said, laughing.

Tun'Gusk stared at them for a long moment, clearing his throat. The rest of the hunters grew silent. "What happened to you, Alynia? I saw that you stopped running, but you were so far away that I couldn't see why. Tapio says he had to knock you out of the way of an angry bull. Did you even see it coming?"

"I didn't see the bull," Alynia admitted.

"What was it then?" asked Tun'Gusk.

Alynia thought Tapio had already told Tun'Gusk what she'd said, so she didn't think it would be a good idea to make up a story or lie about it. She'd seen them talking several times that evening in hushed voices with animated gestures.

"I saw a white buffalo," she said, expecting the rest of the hunters to think that she was making a joke and laugh at her. Instead, they remained silent. She even heard a few take deep breaths. She laughed nervously.

Tun'Gusk stared at her again, studying her face. "Alynia, a white buffalo is not something we speak of lightly. It is not something any of us joke about," he said, standing, his voice growing louder. "Maybe you don't remember this because you are too young or because you're always out playing with birds instead of studying in the village, but the white buffalo is sacred to our people."

"But I really did see a white buffalo. It was a calf," Alynia insisted, her voice cracking a little as she spoke. "Tapio checked my head for..."

"I think that it's time you know why the buffalo is sacred," Tun'Gusk cut her off before she could explain any further. "The white buffalo is the most favored beast of the ancient one, Sehebre. Because our people choose to honor Sehebre and his ways, we also honor the white buffalo in the ways Sehebre would."

"Yes, but..." Alynia tried to interject, but Tun'Gusk glared at her and continued despite her interruption.

"A white buffalo is rare—so rare, in fact, that there has not been a sighting in many, many generations. If you did, indeed, see one, then I will have to tell Nabu, the tribal Mother, and your parents of your sighting. So, as you can see, this is serious."

Tun'Gusk recalled the time when Alynia was born, for he knew that she was a gifted child with potential to change the world. He remembered how the village had celebrated her birth. He was confident that she was telling the truth, especially once

67

he'd witnessed her unique ability to speak with Moonshade in the bird's natural language, but he still had to make sure.

"Swear to me that you are telling the truth," he implored. "Swear to me on the lives of all the birds you love and adore."

"I swear!" she insisted, remembering what Moonshade had said about trusting herself and her vision. She looked at all the other hunters, who sat holding their breath, collectively silent.

Tun'Gusk clasped his hands and nodded his head. "I believe you, young Alynia. We head back to the village at dawn, where we will share this news with everyone, together."

The other hunters cheered, then, applauding this exchange as well as the announcement of their imminent return to the village. They missed their families and homes, just as Alynia did. Tapio and Nakono grinned at her.

Alynia smiled, her belly full of delicious, fresh food. She was delighted that Tun'Gusk believed her and curious about what it meant to have seen such a rare animal. And of course, she was excited about returning to her bed, and soon, her feathered friends.

# Chapter 8

## Heading Home

The journey back to the village was almost as uneventful as the journey away had been, but Alynia kept herself entertained by talking with the other hunters. Tapio was especially helpful, giving her a lesson or two each day on how to improve her running skills. The success of the hunting expedition had everyone in good spirits, and there was much merriment and singing as well as game playing.

On the first afternoon of their journey back, Alynia asked Tomas and Paulo about the game they'd invented that involved the collecting and compiling of stones for use with their slingshots. She'd been curious about it since she first saw them preparing to play it.

Paulo handed a few stones to Alynia. "You should keep your eyes open, as we journey, for good stones in the path. There won't be many this far from the river, of course," Paulo explained, "but I found some excellent ones on the way out. There will be many good stones for you to find once we make it to Red Rock River."

"When will you play the game again?" Alynia asked, because what she wanted was a chance to use a slingshot. It looked as if it would be fun to learn how to use one.

Tomas looked at his brother out of the corner of his eye, a smile breaking across his tanned face. "We can play tonight before dinner, if you like," Tomas said, "if you're willing to wager the berry pie you've been holding on to all week."

Alynia had been saving the pie her father had packed for her because she didn't want to share it with the other hunters. She had just been thinking of eating it, too, to celebrate that the stampeding herd of buffalo hadn't trampled her and that she hadn't ruined the hunting expedition when she'd seen the white buffalo. She thought about the offer for a moment and decided that it was a good wager. The pie would go bad if she didn't eat it soon, anyway, and if she won the wager, she could ask for something in return.

"I'll do it," nodded Alynia, "but only if you're willing to wager one of your slingshots!"

Tomas was surprised by her boldness, his eyes growing wide. "Do you think you have what it takes to beat us at our game, little one?" he asked.

"We'll see!" she shrugged.

So, they agreed to set up a target once they made camp for the night. They'd have the competition just before dinner. The other hunters were excited about the evening's entertainment, but Alynia could tell that they didn't think she would win. She'd have to show them how good she was at games—as soon as she learned all the rules.

Paulo and Tomas found a large stone with a flat top about fifty yards from the campsite and placed both their packs on top of it. Then, they placed a small clay bottle they'd been using to carry water between their packs so it was balanced above the stone but stable.

"For the sake of a fair competition," Paulo began, collecting his pebbles and pouring them into a pile on the ground, "we will all be able to select pebbles in turns. Alynia will have the first turn because she is new at this game."

"Since she's new at this game," continued Tomas, "she can also take two shots for every one of our shots. This will have the added benefit of giving her more practice with our slingshots so she learns how to use them better!" He poured his collection

70

of pebbles into the pile, and then all three began to take turns selecting the pebbles they thought were the best. Once they finished their selections, they showed Alynia the basics of shooting a slingshot while the other hunters gathered around them to watch.

Alynia lined up her first shot, aiming for the bottle as she pulled back on the sling. She'd placed a stone in the sling that she thought was the perfect size and weight to knock down the clay bottle. It was difficult to keep her arm steady because she was excited and confident that she would win the contest. Frumpy and Swiftfeather would be so impressed with her new weapon! She held her breath, just as Paulo had instructed, and then she let the stone fly.

It flew in a wild arc, rapidly curving far to the right of her target and hitting the ground much sooner than she had expected. She tried to ignore the stifled chuckling of the hunters, especially Tomas, who looked forward to devouring the berry pie. Alynia imagined that he'd gobble it in just a bite or two and shook her head, choosing her second stone.

The second shot was better than the first was, but it still fell short of the target. "Your aim is improving already, Alynia," Tapio observed, encouraging her. "You'll

do better on the next round."

Paulo stepped up to the mark they'd made in the dirt, winking at Alynia. "Watch this," he said, lining up his shot. He pulled back on the sling in an effortless, practiced motion, and then let his shot go. The stone flew straight toward the bottle, moving as fast as an arrow fired from a hunter's bow. Alynia stared in surprise as the stone impacted the bottle, shattering it.

"I didn't even get a chance to shoot!" Tomas cried, just as the other hunters erupted into laughter.

Paulo smiled at him, and then turned toward Alynia. "We can share the pie if you want!"

Alynia tried to fight back her tears. She'd been so confident that she could win the contest, ignoring that Paulo and Tomas were much more experienced than she was at using the slingshots. She'd dismissed the fact that it was their game, and now, she would have to give up her dessert because of it. She reached in her bag and found the pie, handing it to Paulo.

"This is going to be delicious!" he said. "Sorry, Alynia, but a wager is binding."

"Did you really think you could beat us?" asked Tomas, unhappy because he hadn't had a chance even to compete.

"I thought that I could make the shot," Alynia offered, still on the verge of tears.

They gathered around the campfire and began to eat their dinner. The fresh buffalo steaks were not as delicious to Alynia, though. She watched as everyone continued to make jokes and tell stories as if nothing had gone wrong. They weren't the ones who had lost their dessert! She thought about it as she ate, and though it was disheartening, Tomas and Paulo were right. She had been foolish and proud. She'd make sure not to make the same mistake again in the future—or at least not wager her only berry pie against professionals.

Tapio came over to Alynia and sat. "The other hunters loved that there was a contest before the meal," he informed her. "They want another one tomorrow. We should be home on the day after tomorrow, so we should have a race before we get back to the village."

Alynia eyed Tapio suspiciously. He was still a faster runner than she was, no matter how much she had improved her skill. His legs were longer, and it took him much more time to run out of breath. He also seemed to have a special ability to move faster than any runner should be able to. Alynia recalled the first race she'd run against him. How had he made it to the finish line, passing her, without her even seeing him?

"I don't know, Tapio," she said hesitantly. "You're a really fast runner. I don't have anything to wager in the contest anymore, either!"

"You don't have to wager anything!" Tapio said. "It will be just for fun! But in order to make it more interesting and competitive for you, I'll offer you a prize if you defeat me." He pulled a multicolored feather from his hair. It sparkled in the firelight like sunlight reflecting off the ripples in a pond.

"That's beautiful!" Alynia observed. It would go well with the feather Frumpy had given her for luck, if only she could win it!

"This feather has magical properties. I'll tell you about them if you win," he said. "Think about it. You have until dinner tomorrow to decide."

"I'll race you tomorrow," Alynia said. "Maybe luck will be on my side, and I'll win the feather."

"Get some rest, little sister. You'll need your energy for the trek home. We're moving faster than normal so we can be back in time for the hunting feast. Everyone is very excited about returning!" He rose and made his way to his sleeping blanket.

Alynia yawned, rolling out her sleeping blanket. As she stretched under the stars, she studied the sky. The constellations Tenderheart had taught her over the years moved across the heavens. She found the constellation Orvieto, and then searched for the Crystal Bear, which was very close in the night sky.

In a few days, the two constellations would cross paths. Every year, just as her birthday arrived, the constellations merged. As she stared at the heavens, she found comfort in recognizing the sign under which she was born. She wondered whether Tenderheart was studying the same celestial dance from her willow.

As her eyelids grew heavy and she dozed off, she started to imagine the faces of her friends at the orphanage in the few clouds that drifted across the night sky. She was fast asleep a few moments later, dreaming of the feast waiting for the hunting expedition, just as the rest of the hunters were. Only Lurs remained awake, silently smoking his pipe, guarding the group from predators in the night and ensuring that the fire did not go out until dawn.

# Chapter 9

## The Final Race

When the first beams of sunlight broke over the horizon, Alynia and the others were already on the move. They took turns with the weight of their buffalo; even Alynia helped pull when the hunters would let her. She didn't want Tapio to think that she was saving all her energy for the race, because he was working just as hard as everyone else was, and they were moving briskly, eager to return to their families and homes.

Sometime around noon, Moonshade landed next to Alynia. She'd been flying around the group, landing occasionally for conversations with Tun'Gusk and Alynia about their village and way of life. This time, she had a somber look in her eyes.

"My new friend, it is time for us to go on our own paths," Moonshade said to Alynia. "My journey is not the same as yours, but I have learned many new things as a result of meeting you."

"Moonshade, you don't have to go," Alynia said. "You can come live at the orphanage and help the young birds. They desperately need older birds to mentor them, because there are more orphans than ever, it seems."

"I will keep it in mind. Tun'Gusk has given me directions to your village so I may find you when I am in the area and want to visit, but I have many more things to learn on my own. As do you, it seems!" The falcon winked at her.

"You mean with the slingshots?" Alynia asked.

"You're a youngling, still. You should always remember that something new can be learned if you keep your eyes and ears open to the world."

"I'm glad that we met!" Alynia said, embracing Moonshade. The hunters all took turns patting the bird on the head or shaking her wing, thanking her for helping them with the buffalo hunt.

"I want you to have this feather as a token of our new friendship," Moonshade said, handing a sleek black feather to Alynia. "May it serve as a memento of the lessons you have already learned and a reminder of the lessons you have yet to encounter." With that, the falcon launched into the sky, flapping her wings with all her strength.

"I'll see you again, won't I?" Alynia called up to the bird, which was already growing smaller in the sky.

"Keep your eyes open, youngling. You have friends everywhere!" the falcon cried back, flying in the direction from which they'd marched.

"She was a regal bird," Kauket said. "I wonder if she was royalty in the land she came from."

"There's no way to tell," Nakono replied. "Anything is possible when it comes to birds, though."

Alynia nodded. "You're right about that!"

They continued their journey toward the village for several more hours, watching the sun make its way across the sky. As the day grew late, the hunters began to talk excitedly about the upcoming race between Alynia and Tapio. The last race had been a close one, and all the hunters had seen how much Alynia had improved her technique during their expedition. On the other hand, they all knew that Tapio was fast, and most suspected that he'd been holding back on the previous race to not discourage the child.

Before she knew it, it was time for the race to begin. Tapio pointed out several objectives for them to reach during their run—a lone tree, far in the distance, followed by a return to the camp, then a long sprint toward a small pond they'd spotted in the distance to the south. The final leg of the race involved running from the pond, uphill, and back to the camp. Alynia wasn't sure about the proper approach because running toward the pond would be the easiest part of the race given that it was slightly downhill. She thought about running as quickly as possible down the hill, using the inclination to help her speed, but didn't want to use all her energy before she had to make it back to the camp. She wanted to ask Tapio what his plan was but didn't want to give away her own.

Instead, she approached Tun'Gusk for advice. "What is the best technique for a race like this?" she asked him.

"I'm no racer," he answered, "but if I were running, I'd consult with Tapio first."

"But he's my competition? What if he lies to me so he can win?"

"Why would he lie to you? Tapio is one of my most trusted friends. Besides, he saved your life in the buffalo stampede!" Tun'Gusk shook his head. "You have a long way to go, child."

That wasn't a good sign. Tun'Gusk was difficult to understand. One moment, he was helpful, and the next, he dismissed her. She knew that he liked her; otherwise, he wouldn't have allowed her to come on the expedition. Maybe he was just hungry. Tun'Gusk always liked to eat.

Next, Alynia approached Nakono. "Nakono, what would you do?" she asked.

Nakono frowned. "Are you sure you want to know? Are you old enough for me to tell you what I'd do?"

Alynia nodded, curious about what Nakono would say.

"I'd find a way to trick him," she continued. "I'd probably get an archer like Lurs to shoot him in the leg so he couldn't run!" she laughed.

Alynia gulped, and her eyes grew wide.

"That is, if Tapio wasn't my friend," Nakono explained. "But because he is, I'd ask him what he was going to do to win and then modify my tactics accordingly. I'd improve my approach with the knowledge of his technique. It's a good way to hunt, too, you know, observing your prey for its migratory patterns, and then making a plan of attack."

Alynia thanked Nakono for the advice, though it wasn't what she wanted to hear. She would have to ask Tapio about his plan for the race after all.

She approached him just before the race. He was stretching his legs in preparation, so she began to mimic his movements. It felt good to stretch her muscles out after all the walking they'd been doing.

"Tapio, which leg of the race should I put the most energy into? Should I run as quickly as possible from the start and try to get the lead, or should I save my energy for one final burst at the end, when you'll be exhausted from running?"

"I'm going to try to evenly distribute my speed over the entire race," he said. "I think that the best technique for a race such as this one is exercising control and moderation and maintaining a steady speed from start to finish. Do you think that your approach will be better?"

She hadn't expected him to ask her about that, thinking that he would not take her ideas for the race seriously. "If you're steady, and I get the lead, then I can go steady after that, and I'll win," she reasoned. "Maybe that's what I'll try."

"Maybe I'll wait for you to do that, though, and if I see that you're winning, in the very end, I'll run past you with the last bits of my energy, winning in the nick of time!"

Tapio would be difficult to beat; Alynia was sure of it. She didn't want to make the same mistake as the day before and assume that she could win from the start, though the last race they'd been in had been close.

"You'll do well, no matter what your approach to the race is," Tapio said, slapping her on the shoulder. "You're an excellent racer—maybe the second best in the expedition!"

Alynia hit him on the arm playfully.

"If you're ready to race, everyone's gathered around us," Tapio said.

"Ready when you are," Alynia answered, looking at the distant tree. This would be like the times she'd raced Frumpy, she thought. It was all in how she looked at things. She couldn't let her worries about losing the race or her wishes for winning cloud her mind while she ran. She cleared the thoughts of everything but her next goal from her mind, just as Tapio had instructed, waiting for Tun'Gusk to signal the start of the race.

Then the signal came, and they were off, bolting toward the tree. Both racers started fast, keeping pace with each other. Alynia applied all the lessons Tapio had given to her; she didn't even kick up a single puff of dust as she rapidly made her way toward the tree that was their goal. They reached the lone tree about the same time, each tapping it in turn, before continuing back toward the hunters.

The hunters began to cheer as Alynia took the lead from Tapio when they were almost back to the camp. She was putting a little more energy into running than she thought she should have, because she could start to feel her legs burning, and she was already breaking a sweat. Tapio seemed content to let her have the slight lead, pacing himself as he'd told her he would. She only had to maintain a slight lead for the rest of the race to win, and the next part of the race would be down toward the pond.

The pond looked cool and refreshing as Alynia approached it, still in the lead. She wanted to swim in the sparkling blue water. Her mind wandered for a moment as she noticed a fish leaping into the air at the far side of the pond. How many fish could she catch here? Would Swiftfeather ever fly this far out to help her catch fish for the orphans? As she approached the shore of the pond, she realized that she'd slowed some during her musings about the fish, and Tapio had passed her!

"See you at the finish line, young one!" Tapio exclaimed, already heading back up the hill toward the camp. The hunters' cheers could be heard all the way down at the pond. They were very excited by the sudden turn of events.

Alynia saved her breath, knowing that answering Tapio would only slow her down. She cleared all thoughts from her head again, determined to win the race. It wasn't only about winning the feather Tapio had offered as a prize; it was important to her because she wanted to show all the hunters that she'd learned something on her journey. She wanted them to approve of her when they returned to the village, because most had scoffed at her on the day they'd first met.

She pushed as hard as she ever had, running with every ounce of energy she could muster. Soon, she was nearing Tapio, closing in on him. A moment later, she was beside him, and if she had turned to look at him, she would have noticed that he had a surprised expression on his face, but she concentrated only on making it to the finish line first.

Tapio began to run faster, regaining the lead, but the race had exhausted him as much as it had Alynia. He knew that he couldn't keep up his pace for the rest of the distance to the finish, but he also knew that Alynia would probably slow soon. Alynia passed him again after a few long strides up the hill. The hunters roared in approval.

Then, she crossed the finish line first, skidding to a halt right in front of Tun'Gusk, who grabbed her up in a swift motion and threw her on his shoulders.

"We have a new champion runner in the expedition!" he announced. "Alynia defeated Tapio! This will become the source of many tales and songs. I'm sure of it!"

The other hunters continued to cheer, some making jokes to Tapio about losing the race.

"Maybe you're getting too old," Tomas said.

"Maybe you're getting too fat!" Paulo added. "Too many buffalo steaks this week!"

Tun'Gusk lowered Alynia from his shoulders, helping her to the ground so she could rest.

Tapio sat beside her. "That was a fantastic competition, Alynia," he said.

"You didn't think I would win, did you?" she asked.

"You didn't think you would win, either, not until the end," he answered. "Here's the feather I promised you. It has magical properties you'll have to remember to use sparingly, because you can only call on them so many times. It used to be much more brilliantly colored than it is now, but I've used it a few times since I got it."

"What are the magical properties?" Alynia asked, turning the beautiful feather over in her hands.

"This feather will allow you to move faster than even the fastest arrow—as fast as a bolt of lightning, even. When you touch the feather and wish to run, it will work. Each time you use it, though, its power diminishes and its colors fade, so save it for when you need it most. It is very valuable."

Alynia was happy to accept the prize, and she considered what Tapio had just told her. "Wait a minute," she said. "The first race against me... is that how you won?"

He winked at her, shaking his head. "It's time to eat." He avoided her question. "I'm starving after a race like that."

Alynia tied the feather to her arm with the other feathers she'd collected. It was the most beautiful feather she'd seen, but it didn't mean as much to her as the feathers she'd received from Frumpy and Moonshade.

The hunters had a light dinner and went to bed early, because they knew that the next day they'd be home, just in time for the village feast. Alynia couldn't see the constellations in the sky as she drifted to sleep, because a group of clouds had covered them as the sun set on the horizon. Instead, she was lulled to sleep by the sound of distant thunder.

# Chapter 10

## A Surprise Ruined

As they approached their village the next day, Alynia grew more and more anxious about getting home in time to see Frumpy. She missed him so! Several times, she ran ahead of the other hunters, who warned her to stay with the party so they could all arrive home at the same time.

"I'll just go ahead and make sure the path is clear," Alynia said, making excuses for running ahead. Each time, she'd go a little farther than before, waiting for the expedition to catch her. She knew the way home, anyway, and because they wouldn't let her help carry the load of buffalo, she didn't see any reason for her to stay. It also looked as if it was going to rain. Dark storm clouds had gathered in the sky during the morning, and the thunder was above them now.

She remembered that the feather she'd won from Tapio could help her move faster, and she was eager to try it, though he'd told her to save it for when she needed it. She wanted to see Frumpy very much, though, so she reached to the feather as she darted ahead.

Her vision blurred as she ran, so she stopped running to orient herself. As soon as she stopped running, her vision cleared, and she discovered that she was already at the village border, but no one had seen or heard her arrive. She'd covered the amazing distance of at least an hour's walking in just a blink of an eye!

She took the magical feather from her armband and examined it, noticing that some color had diminished. Some gray spots that hadn't been there before were scattered among its rainbow of color. *So, that's what Tapio means*, she thought.

"I'll really have to be careful with this in the future," she whispered to herself.

She looked at the villagers going about their business. They were preparing for the return of the hunters, but they were not committed to the task, because they didn't know when the hunters would return. Some village women looked nervously at the sky, worrying that the impending rain would ruin their chances of having the celebration.

Then, she saw her mother coming out from the baker's hut. Her mother carried a huge cake, and Alynia realized that it must have been for her birthday. She ran from her spot in the trees toward her mother, not caring how much dust she kicked up. O'stara almost dropped the cake on the ground. She was so surprised by Alynia's arrival and the huge embrace she received as Alynia threw her arms around her.

"Alynia Sky!" her mother exclaimed. "You're home from the hunt!"

"Mother, I missed you and Father so much!" Alynia said, still hugging O'stara. "I have so much to tell you about the hunting expedition!"

"Are the rest of the hunters on their way?" her mother asked, signaling to the other villagers, who had noticed Alynia's arrival.

"Yes! They should be here soon!"

The villagers began to clap with joy. Everyone was excited that the feast would happen that evening, so preparations began in earnest.

When Tun'Gusk and the others arrived, just over an hour later, Alynia was there to greet them.

"We told you to stay with the group," Tun'Gusk scolded her. She thought he'd be happy to see her. "Where is your father? Where is Nabu? We must speak to them immediately. Go find the village Mother!" he demanded.

She looked at Tapio and the others, but they all seemed angry with her for running ahead. Tapio shook his head in disapproval. "You should do what Tun'Gusk says," he told her. "It is important to follow instructions."

Alynia turned and ran toward her hut as the rest of the villagers passed her, greeting the returning hunting expedition. Why was everyone so mean to her? she wondered. She was only trying to be helpful by announcing their arrival, and she'd used the feather for something good for everyone, not just herself. She missed Frumpy very much.

She thought about the village festival and how everyone would be there. She knew that Tun'Gusk was angry with her for running ahead, and she didn't want to hear his lecture in front of her father, mother, and the rest of the village. Everyone would be watching her, treating her like a child, which would be embarrassing. She would rather eat dinner with her feathered friends at the orphanage, anyway, and she was sure that Swiftfeather had captured enough fish that morning for her to share.

She stopped by her hut, checking whether Frumpy was around, but he was nowhere to be found. After reaching beneath her cot to grab a change of clothes and some berries from the cupboard, she crept back into the street. The entire village was absorbed in preparing the buffalo the expedition had brought home, and no one paid attention to her. She thought about her birthday cake and that it would be delicious but decided that it wouldn't be nearly as good without Poplin on her shoulder to share it and Frumpy at her feet, grabbing the crumbs she threw out for him.

Alynia started making her way toward Red Rock River and Tenderheart's willow. She didn't care anymore whether she missed her birthday. Her friends were more important. The village could celebrate without her.

As she crossed Red Rock River, she noticed that the waters were higher than usual. She looked upstream and saw dark clouds looming in the distance. There were several flashes of lightning in the clouds, but they were far away, so Alynia knew that she had time to make it to the willow before it started raining. As if to signal that it could read her thoughts, the weather began to change over her. Thunder boomed across the water, coming down from the sky above her. It shook the branches of the crooked tree, frightening her a little.

"It's just a storm," she reassured herself. "Nothing to be afraid of!"

The waters of the river tugged at her heels as she tried to cross on some higher rocks, but after a moment of balancing on the slippery surfaces, she gave up and decided to plunge into a deeper part and cross the river by swimming. She held her breath as she dove below the surface, opening her eyes beneath the water so she could see all the shining scales of the fish that lived in the river. If she could have spoken to them, she would have warned them about Swiftfeather, but she was busy holding air inside her, as she fought against the current to make it to the other shore.

When she broke the surface of the river with a splash, Alynia saw that she had been pulled downstream much farther than she thought, but she wasn't worried because she'd be across the river before it took her too far. She made one final dive, waving to an especially large fish as it swam by, and then she climbed from the river onto the far shore. She tried to wring as much water as she could from her clothes, but as she examined the approaching clouds, she thought that it wouldn't do much good to try to get dry. More thunder echoed across the landscape, reaffirming her thoughts on the subject.

Just as she rounded the final bend to Tenderheart's willow, the rain began to fall from the overloaded clouds above. Great torrents of water poured down in the form of giant raindrops, splashing in the dirt, making miniature craters as they hit the ground. It was as if the sky had been holding back all its drops of rain for as long as it could stand, but couldn't hold it anymore, and let everything go at once. After a few minutes of this, the heavy rain diminished and settled into the gentle rainfall in which Alynia loved to play. She looked at the drops as they fell from the sky and smiled.

"That's better," she said, to no one in particular, pleased with the change. "Even if it ruins the celebration back at the village!" She felt smug about the rain falling on the Festival of the Hunt. She didn't want the others having fun, because she believed that they were always trying to stop her from having adventures of her own. She lost track of time as she made her way to the orphanage, and before she knew it, she was just a few hundred paces away.

Frumpy was already running toward her as fast as he could. Alynia bolted toward her friend, taking him up in her arms as they met.

"It's been forever, Alynia!" Frumpy exclaimed. "I missed you so much! None of the birds here are nearly as fun as you are!"

Alynia laughed at her friend, burying her face in his soft, brown feathers. He smelled like fresh, wet hay. She squeezed him as hard as she could without crushing him.

"I've missed you, too, Frumpy! The buffalo hunt was mostly boring, and all I wanted the whole time was for you to be there with me!"

"Did you stay out of trouble?" Frumpy asked, giving her a serious look.

"Mostly!" Alynia chuckled, her resentment of the village fading by the second. "I learned some new tricks for racing, too, so next time we race to Red Rock River, you'll need a huge head start!"

"I'll win one day! Come on!" He jumped from her arms and started toward Tenderheart's willow. "Someone would really like to see you on a day like today!"

86

They arrived at the tree a moment later, making their way past the long, drooping branches and getting deep into the willow. Birds twittered excitedly about Alynia's return, hopping from branch to branch. The willow was still an extremely magical place, and though the rain continued to fall outside the branches, it was mostly diminished at the trunk.

Alynia began to climb into the tree as Frumpy stood beside her, smiling. She noticed that the bark was slick from the rain, but she had a lot of practice climbing into the branches, and she made sure that she had a good grip as she ascended. Once she made it a few branches into the tree, she paused to take in the beautiful sight of the orphanage Tenderheart had founded.

"Do you remember me?" a voiced quietly peeped from just behind Alynia's head. She smiled, instantly recognizing the speaker.

"Poplin! How could I forget you?" Alynia threw her arms out to Poplin, and he jumped across them, skipping excitedly until he reached her shoulder, where he began to nuzzle her neck and ear.

"I thought you might not remember me because you found some new friends while you were away on your expedition," Poplin explained.

"I found some new friends, it's true, but no one would ever make me forget how much I love you, Poplin!"

Poplin chirped a little and then sighed.

"What's wrong? Aren't you excited to see me?" Alynia asked.

"I am," Poplin said. "I'm just sad today because it's raining."

"A lot of birds love to play in the rain! Have you tried it?"

"Playing in the rain is fun, it's true, but today was going to be a special day for me. I was going to take my first flying lesson today from Swiftfeather. He says that the weather isn't good for learning how to fly today, that it's too dangerous for a bird as small as I am. This morning, I said a little prayer when I woke. Today, I was going to ask the sky to teach me how to fly."

Alynia considered this. Swiftfeather was an expert at many things, but she couldn't discern a reason for his statement that Poplin should wait to fly. It wasn't even raining that hard within the branches of the willow. Surely, Poplin could learn something today, even if it was just gliding to the ground!

"Where is Swiftfeather?" Alynia asked, looking around.

"He went to catch some fish before the waters of the river get too deep for him to dive into," Frumpy called up to them. "I'm surprised you didn't see him on your way here. He probably would have asked you to help him spear some fish because you're so good at it!"

"I was distracted when I left," Alynia said. "I didn't bring my spear with me. Maybe I didn't see Swiftfeather because he was fishing farther upriver."

Poplin sighed again in a mighty breath that Alynia didn't think was possible from such a tiny creature. She felt terrible for him. He must have been very disappointed with the weather.

"Today is a special day for me, too, Poplin," she said. "It's my birthday! But everyone in the village was being mean, so I came here to spend it with you and my other friends. You are so much nicer than those villagers!"

Poplin cheered up a bit when she said that, but she could tell that he was still upset about the cancellation of his lessons.

"Tell you what," she offered. "This branch isn't that high. Let's jump down together, and you can try to glide to the ground. Just hold your arms out like this, and then jump." She illustrated by holding her arms out horizontally and then jumping to the ground below.

"See, there's nothing to it!"

Frumpy jumped up and down excitedly. "You can do it, Poplin!" he cheered.

"I don't know. It's really far!" Poplin said nervously.

Alynia climbed back up the trunk of the willow to the branch on which Poplin sat. She noticed that a few other birds had hopped over to watch and thought that they were probably making Poplin more nervous than he should have been about jumping.

"Hey," she called to the gathering flock. "You guys should cheer little Poplin on!"

The other birds began to chirp and cluck and tweet with excitement and encouragement for Poplin, so he puffed out his chest in response, readying himself for his first big leap into the air.

"Alynia, is this how I hold my wings?" he asked, stretching his wings experimentally.

"Yes!" she affirmed, holding her arms out as far as she could. Suddenly, her foot slipped on the wet bark of the branch, and before she knew it, she was falling through the air toward the ground. She put her arms in front of her, trying to brace for impact with the earth below, involuntarily crying out. There was a bright flash of light, like lightning, what seemed like a tremendous clap of thunder, and then there was darkness.

## Chapter 11

## The Vision of Destiny

Alynia opened her eyes and looked around in the darkness of the room in which she lay. She felt her familiar pile of animal furs wrapped around her and realized that she was in the village, in her hut, and in her bed. Poplin's words surfaced in her mind.

"Today, I was going to ask the sky to teach me how to fly."

She closed her eyes as a vision of Poplin crying to the heavens flashed across her mind. His voice echoed the sentence repeatedly. Alynia was drenched in sweat... or was it rain? She wasn't sure. The animal furs of her bed were soaked, though, and she had the thought that her parents would be angry with her if she ruined the furs by sweating all over them.

Her heart pounded, slamming against her chest in rapid and heavy thumping beats. She tried to slow her breathing, using techniques Tapio had shown her while on the expedition. The expedition! She'd forgotten for a moment that there was a festival happening.

She listened for the beating of the celebratory drums, but she couldn't hear anything except thunder... the thunderous booming in her ears of her beating heart. She lifted her head, searching for her parents in the darkness, but they weren't in the hut. Chills shot through her body, and she felt the sweat pour from her skin.

*Why? Why? Why?* she thought, trying to call out and finding that she couldn't. She heard Poplin's voice repeating its mantra. She lifted her hands toward her face, wiping some sweat from her brow.

*How did I get here? Where was I before?* she wondered, trying to follow her memories toward the moment she'd come home. She closed her eyes and began to massage her aching temples, her fingers gliding across her slick skin in swirling motions.

Suddenly, she jolted! Swirls of blue and purple whirled inside her eyelids. She tried to jump up but realized that she couldn't move. She felt a burst of adrenaline from the fear of being immobilized and tried to call for help, but she couldn't.

*Why can't I move?* she thought. *What's happening to me?*

Although she used all her willpower, she couldn't regain control of her body. She lay there, helplessly stuck in place, waiting, and trying to calm herself. Her vision was still overwhelmed with swirling color, and each pounding beat of her heart caused another rippling burst of colors to splash across her eyelids. She began to relax, hypnotized by the swirling rainbow inside her head. She was mesmerized by how vivid the colors were, though she was more frightened than she could ever remember being.

Suddenly, a voice she'd never heard called to her through the myriad colors that filled her vision. "Sky, teach, fly."

Alynia wasn't sure whether the voice came from inside her hut or was only inside her mind, but again, it called to her. "Sky, teach, fly."

"Help me!" she called in response to the strange voice, but she realized that her words never escaped her lips and only echoed through her mind. The brilliant colors continued to swirl while the voice repeated itself, fading to a whisper in the back of her head.

"Sky, teach, fly. Sky, teach fly. Sky, teach, fly."

The colors obscuring her vision began to diminish, and the darkness of the night inside her hut returned. Alynia groaned as she tried to regain control of her body, but she still couldn't move. She tried to call to her parents for help, but she still couldn't use her voice. She relaxed for a moment, resigning herself to wait out whatever was happening to her.

A golden beam of light began to shine through the blackness of the room. Alynia focused on the light and concluded that it was happening in her mind, just as the colors had. She was still having a vision! When she understood that she was in a dream-like state, she began to relax more and accept what was happening to her.

As the light continued to brighten, shapes began to emerge within it. She squinted her eyes, trying to understand what she saw. Some time passed, but she couldn't be sure whether it had been hours or just seconds. Suddenly, it became clear to her—she was looking at a sunrise coming over the rock formations of Sehebre's Finger!

"Sky, teach, fly!" The mysterious voice commanded her one final time. The colors, light, and voice faded into blackness, and Alynia sighed, alone and shaken by the vision she'd had.

Then, she remembered how she'd fallen from Tenderheart's willow, trying to teach Poplin how to fly. She slowly raised herself from the damp pile of animal furs in her bed, happy that she could move again. She checked her arms and legs to make sure that they weren't broken. She stretched her limbs, noting the various bruises.

"Nothing serious," she said to herself, jumping out of the bed. "But how did I end up back in the hut?" She quickly made her way out of the hut and into the dark, wet night outside. The rains had become worse during the evening, and the steady downpour drenched her almost immediately, chilling her to the bone. Where were her parents? Where were Frumpy and Poplin?

Thunder loudly cracked across all Ka'lanna. Standing in the darkness and the torrents of rain, Alynia dropped to her knees, looking into the black sky above her. The sweat from her vision washed away as she scanned the sky, searching for an explanation. She hardly noticed the mud splashing up from the ground with every heavy drop of water that came down.

"Sehebre!" she cried toward the heavens. "Why do you torment me?"

She shivered as the cold of the water and the night began to set in on her. She began to cry, and her tears joined the rivulets of water as they made their way across her face, down her body, and onto the earth. She crossed her arms tightly and attempted to hold her warmth in, slowly rocking in place.

"Sehebre!" she called again. She slammed her fist into the ground, splashing large clumps of mud into the air and across her face and chest. Brilliant lightning was followed by a huge clap of thunder, one of the loudest she'd heard. Secondary lightning flashes speckled the clouds above her in response to the thunderclap, like luminous fireflies buried in billowing puffs of smoke. Alynia quickly jumped to her feet, focusing on a single point of light pushing through the clouds above her.

"Is that...?" she muttered. "Could it be?" It was difficult to believe what she saw, but she was sure that it wasn't another lingering remnant of her vision. "It really is true! It's Venus!" she exclaimed. Far above her in the Northern Sky, barely shining through the heavy clouds, was Venus.

Serenity found its way into Alynia, and her mind was set at ease again. She stopped crying and began to wipe the mud from her arms and cheeks in rhythmic motions. With her eyes still locked on Venus above her, she began to walk backward until she ran into the side of her hut. She slowly slid down the exterior wall of her home as she stared at the star above her in the sky, still barely glimmering through the rainclouds, and then she smiled. *Everything will be all right*, she thought. A supremely positive feeling overtook her heart as she fell asleep in the rain, feeling at peace, even in the stormy conditions.

Alynia awoke the next morning and discovered that she was again in her bed. She stretched her arms as she usually did and immediately felt a warm hand on her forehead. She opened her eyes and saw that her mother and father were sitting beside her bed, watching her.

"Alynia, try not to move," her mother said comfortingly. There was a look of concern on her father's face that she'd rarely seen.

"What's the matter? Is everything OK?" Alynia asked.

"You had quite a fall out of the willow," her father said, rubbing the whiskers on his chin. "I had to cross Red Rock River in a torrential downpour just to get to you. Thanks to your rooster friend."

Alynia was confused. She didn't know that her father knew how to speak in the language of birds, but she knew that Frumpy couldn't speak the human language—even if he did understand it.

"How did Frumpy tell you that I fell?" she asked, searching the room for her friend. She was relieved to see him sitting at the foot of her bed. He also wore a concerned expression.

"It wasn't easy!" he clucked.

"That bird made the most noise I've ever heard a creature make," Nak'te explained. "I thought he was going insane, trying to get me to follow him like he did. I finally understood that something was wrong when you were nowhere to be found, but your rooster friend was so vocal. And just in time! The storms got really bad at the willow after I picked you up and carried you home!"

Alynia had a moment of worry about her friends at the orphanage. She remembered what Poplin said about wanting to learn how to fly, and then her vision from the night before came back to her.

"Is everyone at the willow OK?" she asked Frumpy.

"They've seen worse storms than that. Tenderheart's got a kind of magic spell on the place too; I'm sure they're fine," Frumpy reassured her.

94

She turned to her parents. Her mother brushed a strand of hair from Alynia's brow, smiling.

"I had the strangest vision last night," Alynia told them. "It was so powerful that I went outside into the rain and called on Sehebre for answers!"

Her parents looked at each other in earnest and then turned back to Alynia. "Alynia, you haven't left this bed for two days," O'stara said. "I fed you stew and water with a spoon when I could, but you seemed delirious and didn't even know who I was!"

"But that's impossible," Alynia replied, looking down at her clean clothes and skin. "I was just outside in the rain. The mud splashed all over my arms, legs, and face! I even saw Venus shining through the clouds above me. My vision showed me Sehebre's Finger, and I heard a voice speak to me. Do you think something important is at Sehebre's Finger?"

Her father and mother were silent for a moment, exchanging glances. Even Frumpy seemed unsure of what to say to her. Was she going crazy? Had she imagined it all?

Nak'te spoke first, clearing his throat. "Alynia, Tun'Gusk and the other hunters told us about your vision of the white buffalo on the hunting expedition. It is a great sign. After you abandoned the village to spend time with the birds—the ones I now realize truly are your friends, ones you can speak with even—your mother and I had a long discussion with Nabu about what was happening with you."

Alynia didn't like the sound of that. It seemed that her father was going to reprimand her for running away again.

"While it is unfortunate that you missed your surprise birthday celebration on the evening of the great buffalo festival," he continued, "we aren't angry with you."

"As a matter of fact, we want to apologize for discouraging you from pursuing your dreams," her mother interjected. "It seems that you have a great destiny to fulfill, and we want you to know that we are proud of you."

95

"You have always been a strong-willed child, Alynia," her father resumed. "I am proud that you are learning to use your will and interests toward bettering yourself. Your new friend Tapio had many complimentary things to say about you and your performance during the expedition."

"So, you believe me about my dream?" Alynia asked. It seemed too good to be true. It seemed that her parents never believed her about anything... but to be fair, she did have quite an imagination and always made up stories with which to entertain Frumpy and her other friends.

"You never left, but you were in a feverish state for a full day and a full night," O'stara said. "If you had a vision, then we believe that your vision was important. You are quickly becoming a woman, Alynia. Sometimes, it is difficult for parents to trust the word of their children, because it means that the time is quickly approaching to let their children leave the nest and go out into the world, making their own lives and fates."

"I love you, Mom and Dad!" Alynia exclaimed, throwing her arms around her parents and holding them tightly. She felt better than she'd felt in a long time. She reached for Frumpy, who hopped closer and joined the family in the embrace for a moment, but backed away when he thought that he heard Nak'te growling about his being too close.

"Now, we must sleep, Alynia," her mother said. "We have been awake beside you for days. You should sleep more if you can, just to make sure that you are well."

"I would really like to go outside and play with Frumpy for a while," Alynia requested, "if that's OK."

"Don't go far. You aren't fully recovered from your accident. It is still raining, too, so don't try to climb any trees to talk to birds, either!" Nak'te said.

"OK! Sleep well!" Alynia exclaimed, hopping up. She knew that her parents would be asleep in just a few moments, and she planned to go a little farther than she was supposed to go while they slept. The words of Poplin kept surfacing in her memory, along with the voice from her vision. "Sky, teach, fly." "Today, I was going to ask the sky to teach me how to fly."

Alynia and Frumpy went outside in the rain, jumping into puddles as they walked. She knew that something important waited for her at Sehebre's Finger, but she wasn't sure what it would be. There was only one way to find out!

"Frumpy, I have to go up the mountain toward Sehebre's Finger," Alynia told her friend.

"That's not a good idea!" Frumpy protested. "The weather is terrible! You've been asleep for days!"

"I've never felt better, you silly rooster," Alynia said, shoving him into an especially muddy pool of water. "Mother and Father are asleep. It's now or never!"

"Your parents just said that they trusted you and told you not to go far. Sehebre's Finger is really far away!"

"That's why I need your help, Frumpy. I need you to sneak back into the hut and grab my favorite bag for me. You can do it much more quietly than I can. Once you get it, put whatever food you can find in it, and bring it to me near the edge of the village. I have to go to Nabu's for a moment before I meet you!"

Frumpy shook his head, resigning himself to her plan. He knew that she wasn't going to change her mind.

"What do you need at Nabu's?" he asked, curious about her plan.

"You'll see. Just meet me at the edge of the forest path leading up into the mountains." She winked at him conspiratorially and then ran toward Nabu's hut.

She arrived a few minutes later, creeping up to Nabu's home as quietly as she could. She discovered that he was away, just as she suspected he would be, and entered into the building, searching around the room for a very specific prize. When she saw Nabu's sacred feathers hanging from a peg on the wall, she lunged for them, taking them from their decorative resting place and turning on her heel in a single fluid motion. She bolted from his hut as quietly as she could, trying to contain her nervousness. She had heard villagers speaking of Nabu's incantations, and she thought that it was possible for him to have cast a guardian spell on his belongings. She hoped that there wasn't a spell on the house, but if there was, she joked to herself, he must have been blind.

She followed the path away from Nabu's toward the mountains as she tied the feathers to her arms.

"Why are you wearing Nabu's sacred feathers like that?" Frumpy asked her when she arrived at the village gates. "They're sacred! They're not toys for you to play with!"

"If I have these magical feathers on my arms, I'll be more like a bird," she reasoned to him. "Then, even if it rains, I can teach my friends to fly—and maybe even fly with them! I just need to practice more. It's just the same as racing. Tapio told me that all I needed to do is practice, and I'll get better at whatever I try to do!"

"You're so creative!" Frumpy complimented her. "I didn't think of it that way. Maybe that makes it OK that you're using the feathers. Just be careful not to damage them, and put them back where you found them. Nabu isn't someone I'd want to make angry!"

"Even the return of Xoplantah wouldn't stop me from doing what I love!" Alynia declared. A flash of lightning crossed the distant horizon. A low rumble of thunder echoed across the village. She looked up toward Sehebre's Finger.

"I have to go find out what my vision means, Frumpy. You can come with me if you want."

"I probably should come with you, just to make sure you stay out of trouble," he answered, nudging her favorite bag in her direction, "but I'm concerned about the orphanage. It hasn't stopped raining for days, and I wonder how they're holding up there."

Alynia nodded her head, picking up the pack and looking inside. It was filled with delicious berries, fresh bread, and dried fish.

"I understand. I will go to Tenderheart's as soon as I get back from the cliffs above. Thanks for grabbing my pack for me and filling it with such delicious-looking morsels. You know everything I like the best!"

"You'll need your energy to climb those cliffs," Frumpy warned. "Don't forget to take a break whenever you feel tired."

"I'll be back before you know it, Frumpy," Alynia said, playfully shoving her friend again. "This isn't some extended hunting expedition like last time."

"I'll tell Poplin that you miss him," Frumpy said, waving his wing at her.

# Chapter 12

## Answers

Alynia started walking at a brisk pace up the path leading into the mountains, and ultimately, toward Sehebre's Finger. The air was fresh and clear, cleansed by the days of rain, and she didn't even notice that the downpour was unrelenting, soaking her to the bone, because she was so determined to reach the top of the mountain and discover what her vision meant. Her parents would be angry, but they'd understand once she explained. The words kept repeating in her mind. The words she heard were more important than temporarily disobeying her mother and father. She had to know what they meant. "Sky, teach, fly." Each step she took carried her closer and closer to the answer.

Alynia spent most of the morning hiking up the mountain paths leading to the cliffs above the village. Once she made it to the cliffs, she stopped, staring in amazement at what she saw around her. Sehebre's Finger loomed over her in the rain, ominous in the dark shadows of the rainclouds above it.

Below her, whenever lightning flashed across the skies, she saw the hills and trees she'd passed on her journeys. The landscape stretched in every direction, fading into the soft gray of the rain and mist as it blanketed the world. She could see her village below, and it seemed almost too tiny to be real. She tried to find the crooked tree at Red Rock River, but the sheets of rain falling from above obscured her line of sight. She returned her attention to Sehebre's Finger, knowing that she would have to be careful on the rest of her climb. The trail she had been following ended soon.

She made a quick snack of some pastries Frumpy put in her bag and wondered how he'd been able to sneak so many types of food into her pack without being caught. She knew that it was difficult for him to carry things because of the shape of his wings, but she also admired his endless determination when it came to doing things to which he set his mind.

In the end, she dismissed her curiosity, focusing instead on her immediate goals. She looked down at her arms, admiring the bright colors of Nabu's sacred feathers. She imagined that she was a bird, like her friends, and she was soaring through the skies with Tenderheart, Poplin, Swiftfeather, and Moonshade. Maybe she could even teach Frumpy to fly, though she was sure he'd need to lose a bit of weight if he wanted to get very far off the ground.

"Sky, teach, fly." The words came back to her, bringing her out of her imagination and back to reality.

Alynia began to climb the steep and sharp rocks leading to the top of Sehebre's Finger. She'd never been so high in the mountains before; she was higher than even the forest. She'd made excellent speed up the mountain pathways, even in the rain. She smiled, focusing on finding the best places for leverage as she climbed. Her fingers gripped the crags and nooks of the rocks, and her feet anchored her securely in unlikely crevices as she steadily progressed higher and higher.

About two hours later, she reached the plateau of Sehebre's Finger, dragging herself over the muddy ledge onto the flat surface at its peak. She caught her breath, staring into the clouds above for just a few moments, letting the cool rain run over her face and body. The clouds were so close to her now that she felt as if she could touch them.

"Maybe I can bring one of you home with me and show you to Frumpy," she said aloud, speaking to the clouds. She laughed, because she knew that it was impossible to catch a cloud, though it seemed like an excellent idea. She stood and stretched her arms toward them, jumping as high as she could, watching her fingers disappear into the mist above her head. She didn't fear the distant thunder she heard. It even seemed that the storms were clearing away, because the more she jumped toward the clouds, the more they moved away from her, playing some game of chase.

She began to flap her arms as she jumped, copying the motions of different birds she'd seen when they began to fly. She looked down at Nabu's sacred feathers as they lifted and fluttered in the wind and felt a deep sense of peace come over her.

"This is what I want to do forever," she said, promising herself to keep trying to fly until she could. Why should she be limited by her lack of natural wings? If Tapio's magical feather could help him run in an instant anywhere he wanted to be, surely other feathers and incantations could help her soar through the sky!

Suddenly, a whispering voice was carried in by the wind. "The King of Birds," the faint voice uttered, almost indistinguishable in the breezes crossing the top of Sehebre's Finger.

Alynia thought she might be hearing things, so she stopped jumping, slowed her breathing, and tilted her head in the direction from which she thought she heard the words come. She stepped backward and looked around, but she didn't see anyone.

"Is anyone there?" she called. There was no reply; there was only the wind as it passed over the nearby cliffs. Alynia shrugged, thinking that her imagination had gotten the best of her; when suddenly, she heard the whisper again!

"The King of Birds," repeated the voice.

This time, she was sure someone was on the plateau, playing a practical joke on her. She looked around again, but there was nowhere for someone to hide. The surface of Sehebre's Finger was worn smooth by countless years of wind and rain. There were no trees or caves for someone to hide in, so she moved to the precipice of the cliffs and peered over the ledge. There was no one hiding below her, either.

102

"Hello?" Alynia called out. "This isn't funny!"

She waited a moment, and when no response came, she decided that the best thing to do next was to question the mysterious voice traveling on the wind.

"Who is the King of Birds? Where can I find this king?" she called.

To her surprise, the voice immediately replied. "When the stars are above and the stars are below, the ground will meet the sky. Go there, and you will find the King of Birds."

Excitement filled Alynia. This had to be the answer she sought! This voice and its message about the King of Birds had to be connected to what she'd envisioned. She was extremely happy that Sehebre had answered the questions she'd asked him. What other explanation could there be?

*This is my destiny*, Alynia thought. *This is what I need to do. I need to find the King of Birds. Maybe he's the one who keeps repeating the words "sky, teach, fly" to me!*

She was so excited that she didn't notice that the rains had stopped. The clouds were thinning rapidly, carried away into the distance on warm winds. She smiled and stepped to the edge of Sehebre's Finger, stretching her arms horizontally as far as she could. She stared out at the world around her. She'd never realized how big the world was until she'd been so far above it. Nabu's sacred feathers began to glimmer like gemstones, reflecting the sudden beams of sunlight that began to break through the clouds.

"Nabu!" Alynia exclaimed, realizing that she needed to share the story of her vision and her journey up the mountains with him. He could advise her about the deeper meanings of what she'd seen and heard. She didn't bother to untie the feathers from her arms, as excited as she was to speak to him. She began to climb back down the cliffs as fast as she could, descending from the rocks to the mountain pathways in record time. She kept her urgent pace all the way through the hills and forest until she reached the village around two hours later. As soon as she arrived at the border of her village, she began to make her way toward Nabu's hut, running and weaving through the streets, taking shortcuts between houses and behind barns.

Alynia was so determined to see Nabu that she passed him on the way to his hut. Fortunately, Nabu saw her and was curious about where she was going in such a hurry, so he decided to follow her. Alynia arrived at his hut, calling for him, but he stayed behind her a little way, waiting to see what she would do.

Alynia was still excited and curious, so she leaned forward into Nabu's hut, peeking inside.

As she was leaning in, Nabu called from behind her. "What are you doing with my sacred feathers tied to your arms, Alynia?"

Alynia spun around, seeing Nabu standing behind her, arms crossed over his chest, staring at her with concern. She didn't bother to answer his question. Instead, she began to tell him all about the wind and her vision, the message whispered in the sky, about Poplin and her fall from the tree, about the white buffalo she'd seen on the hunt, and how the stars would meet the sky at the King of Birds. Alynia's words were so mixed up and excited that Nabu couldn't make any sense of what she tried to tell him. He uncrossed his arms, looking down at Alynia.

"Why don't we go inside, have some tea, and talk?" he requested gently.

Alynia followed Nabu into his hut. He grabbed two bearskins from one of his storage shelves and placed them across from each other on the floor. He went to his fireplace, retrieved a pot of tea already simmering over the coals, then shuffled over to his pantry and took down two glazed clay sipping cups. He sat on a bearskin and nodded at Alynia, signaling her to do the same. Nabu took his time crossing his legs and adjusting to sitting on the floor, pausing every moment or so to sip his tea. Alynia sipped her tea respectfully, but mostly because she was thirsty after her long run up and down the mountain. She didn't especially enjoy the bitter taste of the roots and leaves Nabu had brewed.

When he was finally situated, Nabu looked at Alynia for a time, examining her. He finally nodded. "My child, now, you may tell me your story."

Again, Alynia began to ramble too fast for Nabu to follow coherently. He sat patiently, trying to piece together her story, listening to her excitement, which gushed in her words and her body language. The words poured from her like an open floodgate.

"Alynia!" Nabu finally shouted. "Calm down."

She paused, catching her breath. "I'm sorry; I'm just so excited that I heard the voice, that I had the vision, and that I've realized what I want to do with my life!" she explained.

"That's fine, child, but you should start at the beginning. Your story doesn't make sense."

Alynia gathered her thoughts for a few minutes while Nabu stared at her and sipped his tea.

She began to calmly tell Nabu about everything that had happened to her on the cliffs of Sehebre's Finger. She didn't leave out a single detail, and Nabu could see the excitement in her eyes as she recounted the story with fiery passion. She told the story of the white buffalo, how she kept hearing the words "sky, teach, fly" echo in her head, and how she had fallen from the tree trying to teach Poplin to fly. When she finished, Nabu smiled at Alynia, then closed his eyes and lowered his head. He contemplated what advice he should give her. After a few deep breaths, he lifted his head and opened his eyes.

"I knew this day would come," he told her in a deep and serene voice.

"What do you mean?" she asked.

Nabu paused, considering his next words. "Things were very different for our people long ago... long before you were born. It was a dark time in our people's history. It was the time of Xoplantah—a never-ending rainstorm."

Alynia's eyes widened at the mention of Xoplantah because she'd always used the word casually whenever it rained. Nabu's tone was quite serious, though, and carried a current of darkness in it that surprised her.

"Yes, child, I know that you and many other villagers joke about Xoplantah. Don't worry, for I am not judgmental."

"You said never-ending?'" Alynia asked. "How long was the rainstorm, really?"

"The rains of Xoplantah drowned our lands for as long as the oldest members of the tribe could remember."

"That has to be a long time," Alynia said.

"It's quite a long time, of course," Nabu replied, "but there is more to the story than just the rains. Sit back and listen. No more interruptions!"

Alynia pressed her lips tightly, holding back the urge to ask more questions. She was still excited about her vision. She wanted to talk more about it, and as interesting as Nabu's story was, she couldn't see how it connected with her life. She looked at the leaves floating in her tea and began swirling them around with her finger, recalling the swirls of color in her vision. Nabu began to tell his story, and Alynia returned her attention to his weathered face.

"One day, a long time ago, it started raining. It rained so fiercely and with such intensity that even the birds could not fly away. The downpour was of such a scale that our hunters could not go on expeditions, and the local farmers could not go out in search of fruit, vegetables, or fish. Weeks passed, and the waters of Xoplantah were unrelenting.

"In desperation, the tribe's elders asked me to lead the people in a ceremony... an incantation that would beckon to the spirit of Sehebre, imploring him to help by causing the rains to abate. For days, I led our tribe in song and dance as we prayed. Afterward, everyone was exhausted."

Nabu shook his head. "I remember it as if it were only yesterday. I returned to my hut for rest. I walked in and began to hang up my ceremonial robes. Soon after, I fell into a deep slumber, which is where you come into the story."

"I thought you said that this happened long before I was born!" Alynia interrupted, unable to contain herself.

He chuckled to himself, appreciating her insight. "You weren't born!" he continued. "While I slept, I had a powerful vision. Sehebre came to visit me in my dreams. He appeared to me in the form of a white buffalo, which has long been a sacred animal in our tribe. In my vision, Sehebre was grazing in the fields by our village. The sky above him was clear, and the crops were bountiful. He lifted his head and gazed at me for an immeasurable time. Although he did not speak, I could hear his words in my mind as if he were inside my head—that soon, a child would be born, that the child would restore balance to the land and one day become the leader of the tribe."

Nabu's eyes began to well with tears as he recounted his vision to Alynia. He reached out and placed his hand on her shoulder, sending chills through her body.

"Alynia," he said, "You were the child Sehebre spoke of."

"I don't understand!" Alynia protested. "How do you know? Why has no one in the village told me this story before? Why haven't you told me yourself?"

"The time has not been right, young one," Nabu answered softly. "You had to find your way to the knowledge on your own."

"My vision?" Alynia asked.

"Let me explain, for there is even more to the story," Nabu said, dismissing her question. "Many months passed since I shared my vision with the elders of the tribe. Child after child was born, yet the rains of Xoplantah still plagued our land. By the end of the year, the council of elders began to disbelieve my dream, saying that I was not well. They dismissed my advice and grew desperate. Some even began to discuss heading south to new lands. I held on to my faith, though, and I was soon rewarded. You, the child of my vision, were born and..." He broke

107

off for a moment; tears began to roll down his cheeks. Then he smiled a joyful smile and continued.

"At the exact moment of your birth, the clouds above us broke apart, and the rains ended. The entire tribe was grateful to you for returning the balance of sun and rain to our lands. In your honor, a weeklong celebration was held. During this time, the name Alynia Sky was chosen for you. Your father and I carried you to the top of Sehebre's Finger, and we called your name in unison, announcing you to the world. Our voices echoed across the plains and over the distant rolling hills. Across our land, the words 'Alynia Sky' resonated within every tree and rock. They resonated in the heart of every creature.

"That is when the birds took flight again, because for years, the rains kept them grounded. As your name reached their ears, they took to the sky to rejoice in your honor."

Alynia was very excited by Nabu's story. She leaned closer to him so she wouldn't miss a word, her eyes growing wider and wider.

"There were big birds, small birds, song birds, and birds of prey. They all danced together in the sky, Alynia. I wish that you could remember that far back, because it is something I will never forget."

Nabu placed his hands on the sides of Alynia's face. "The sky! The sky!" he exclaimed. "The array of colors swirling, dancing, and flying. It was one of the happiest moments of my life. I was very lucky to witness it."

Alynia could almost see Nabu's memories, and he willed her to go back with him to the day that all the birds flew as one, dancing through the heavens. Nabu released Alynia's head and gently placed his hands on his knees.

He took several deep breaths, calming himself, and then added, in what was barely more than a whisper, "Ever since then, you've had a natural kinship with all winged creatures."

Alynia leaned away from Nabu, her eyes still wide. Her mind was filled with disbelief. *Why was this kept from me?* she

108

thought. *Why would no one in the village tell me about such a wonderful event?*

"The council agreed that we should wait until you were grown to tell you about it, Alynia. As I said, you had to find your way," Nabu said, answering her thoughts.

"Nabu, I didn't say anything," Alynia said. "How did you know what I was thinking?"

Nabu hesitated, realizing that he had revealed one of his abilities to her. He silently contemplated what he would say to her as she stared at him expectantly. Finally, he answered her.

"There are mystical things in this world, Alynia, more than you will ever know. Things that are seen and things that are not seen." He paused, carefully piecing together his explanation because he knew that what he said next could change the course of Alynia's life and possibly the destiny of all Ka'lanna. "You have the potential to become something great. You have been blessed by Sehebre himself since birth."

"So it was Sehebre that came to me in my vision?" Alynia asked.

"A dream is a very powerful thing, as is a vision. Follow your heart, child, and walk the path meant for you and for you alone. You know what no other can tell you; even I can't fully explain what Sehebre's message to you means. But you will know in the depths of your soul what the path is, even if your mind or others' advice gets in the way and obscures that path from time to time."

Emotions began to swirl inside Alynia as Nabu's advice settled within her. The reality of everything she'd known so far was coming apart, it seemed, and everything he had just told her about the day she was born and the rains of Xoplantah was overwhelming. She knew what she had to do. She had to travel to where the ground and the sky met, just as her vision and the whispers she'd heard had instructed her.

*Where is it? What do I do when I get there?* she thought.

"Travel west until you come across Teetering Rock. Whatever direction it points is the direction you should travel in," Nabu answered, reading her mind again.

His smile turned into a scowl after that. "Now, it is time for you to leave my hut. I must prepare for my daily incantations that began in the morning. The rains have stopped my burning of incense and herbs throughout the village for the past few days. I must resume the prayers as soon as possible!"

Alynia rose, stretching her arms and legs. "Thank you for your insight, Nabu," she said, bowing slightly. "And thank you for the tea," she added. Then, she bolted through the door of Nabu's hut, running over the footpaths in the village as fast as she could.

## Chapter 13

## The Journey Begins

"Frumpy!" she called, searching for her friend.

She was in luck because Frumpy had returned to the village at some point in the afternoon, and he was just settling down for a nap. He jumped from his nest as soon as he heard his name, looking around in every direction. Alynia blazed past him, making him feel a little dizzy.

"Come on, Frumpy!" she called to him, waving for him to follow her. He leaped to his feet and began to run after her, knowing that without a head start, he could never catch her. He hoped that she would stop for a rest and give him a chance to close the gap between them.

"Mother! Father!" Alynia cried as she continued her rapid circle through the village. There was no response from either of her parents. Alynia continued to call the names of everyone she knew and loved—her entire tribe. With every name she called, her heart beat a little faster.

One by one, everyone stopped whatever task he or she was doing. The hunters who had gathered in the south of the village began to rush toward Alynia. The children, returning from their play in the rolling hills, began to move in her direction. Tanners and fishers from Red Rock River put down their equipment and started running toward her, hearing their names called from an impossible distance, carried by the magic and excitement of Alynia Sky. Even the tribe's Mother, as old and frail

111

as she was, began to move as quickly as she could toward Alynia, who rapidly approached the village gates in the west.

"I am coming, Alynia!" O'stara called as she rushed away from her early posting at the village fires.

Alynia looked over her shoulder as she heard her mother's voice. She stopped at the western gates, collecting her breath, and a moment later, her mother rounded the corner, smiling as Alynia had never seen her smile before. More and more villagers appeared, gathering around Alynia. They all smiled, filled with joy and cheer. Alynia felt very shy at all the attention, and she was somewhat embarrassed that she'd not known about her birth, as most adults of the village had.

Tapio, Tun'Gusk, and the other hunters came to her side, bowing low and somberly, filled with a respect for her she felt that she didn't deserve. Frumpy bounced around the bend as fast as he could, and to Alynia's joy, many birds from Tenderheart's willow began to circle above her. Her eyes filled with happy tears as a special friend descended from the flock.

"Poplin!" Alynia exclaimed. "You learned to fly after all!"

"I listened to what you said, Alynia!" Poplin replied. "I just ignored the part about how to get started by landing on your head!"

Alynia laughed with her friend while her mother and the other villagers smiled self-consciously, confused by the exchange taking place in bird-speak.

"We are all proud of you, my daughter," O'stara said, embracing Alynia. "We have all believed in you since you were born."

"Why didn't Father take me seriously about being friends with the birds?" Alynia asked, looking up into her mother's eyes.

Her mother started to answer, but she was interrupted by Nak'te himself who had joined the procession silently.

"I have always believed in you, too, Alynia Sky. You are the best daughter a father could ever desire, even if you are

112

frustrating at times. I only wanted you to learn the sacred rites and gain insight into the ways of our world from Nabu so you would be better prepared to deal with whatever comes your way in the future. I had to be stern to make sure you were on the right course and to be assured that you developed discipline. You will need discipline and knowledge in the future in any number of situations I will not be able to protect you from!" He hugged Alynia with all his might, his muscular arms squeezing the air right out of her.

"Dad! I... can't... breathe!" Alynia squirmed playfully.

"I, too, doubted that Nabu's prophecy was the truth," Tun'Gusk added. "Until I learned of your vision of the white buffalo, of course, and I saw how quickly you adapted to life during the expedition. Now, I firmly believe in you, with the rest of my band of hunters!" He clapped his hands as loud as thunder, and all the hunters began to cheer, hooting as loudly as they could.

The other villagers joined in the raucous noisemaking, throwing Alynia on their shoulders to celebrate her realizations. Even the children, too young to understand what was happening, began to run in circles around Alynia, throwing wildflowers they'd found into the air. It was all too magical for Alynia to believe.

As the villagers' voices began to die down, Nabu climbed on top of an old tree stump nearby, addressing the crowd. "As you know and as was prophesied," he called, "Alynia Sky, daughter of the Goodwind Tribe, child of Nak'te and O'stara, has been blessed by Sehebre! Alynia received a sign today, one that will guide her as she travels into the unknown to pursue her dream. As soon as she realized this destiny, the rains ceased, just as before, just as on the day she was born unto us!"

Another great cheer rose from the crowd, and Nabu smiled at Alynia, patiently waiting for the noise to diminish. "She will soon embark on her journey, but first, let us support her and honor her in celebration!"

Again, the crowd began to cheer and dance, right there at the western gates of town. Alynia was speechless. So many people approached her and whispered wishes to her that it all became a blur.

113

Nabu approached her after a time, pulling her away from the reveling villagers. "Our blessed child," he began, handing her a package wrapped in red cloth. "I offer you this, the sacred staff of Sehebre. May he always be with you on your quest!"

Alynia reached toward Nabu, taking the staff in her hand and unwrapping it reverently. At the moment it passed from his hands to hers, a new wave of energy passed through the villagers, who began to cheer with renewed fervor.

As she took in the celebrations, she smiled, spotting a group of the hunters: Tapio, Tomas, and Paulo.

She called to them, and they made their way toward her, shaking hands with and clapping villagers on their shoulders as they passed. The hunters were the most enthusiastic of the revelers by far.

"I believed in you all along, little sister," Tapio said, smiling down at her. "Make sure you put the feather I gifted you to good use only in the most important of situations."

"Of course, Tapio!" Alynia replied, shaking his hand. "Thank you for teaching me how to be a better runner. I'll practice racing while I'm away from the village. I promise!"

Tomas spoke next, nudging his brother as if to remind him of something. "We wanted you to have this," he said, as Paulo pulled a slingshot from his satchel. "You did well the first time you used it, but you will need more practice if you are to become a master like us."

Alynia's eyes grew wide. She couldn't believe how kind everyone was. Her heart overflowed with love for her village. "Thank you, Tomas! Thank you, Paulo!"

"Here are some of the best stones I have ever collected," Paulo said as he passed a small pouch of shooting stones to Alynia.

"Maybe you can win my dessert away from me the next time we wager!" Tomas suggested.

114

"We're all very proud of you, Alynia," Tapio said, and the hunters nodded. "The rest of the hunters feel the same way we do, so we speak on their behalf. They are taking their celebrations very seriously, though, so we should go find them and make sure they are not getting too rowdy."

Tapio, Paulo, and Tomas all bowed slightly in front of Alynia, then turned and rejoined the rest of the celebration.

As Alynia watched them go and continued to look at her neighbors, she noticed her father and mother some distance away, staring at her and smiling peacefully. She approached her parents, noting the small bowl her father held in his hands.

"I love you both," Alynia said, excitedly wrapping her arms around them and giving them the biggest bear hug she could muster. "You have taught me many things."

Nak'te smiled at his daughter proudly. He knelt in the dirt and began to mix some dirt with dyes and water already in the bowl in his hands. He began to paint Alynia's face in the traditional colors of their family and village. When he finished, he stepped back and looked into his daughter's eyes. Alynia could feel love radiate from him. With their eyes still locked, he placed his hands on her shoulders. Then, he spoke.

"These are the markings of our tribe. Wear them with pride and know that your tribe is always with you in your heart."

Alynia could feel her heart swelling, but she wasn't sure how to respond, so she hugged him again, holding him as tightly and as closely as she could. A moment later her mother joined them in their embrace.

After several minutes, Alynia stepped away from her parents and began to back toward the woods. Her mother and father both wore bittersweet expressions on their faces.

"Don't worry about me. I have everything I need in my heart and in my mind. I've also got the Staff of Sehebre!"

Her father laughed at her. "Don't forget this," he said, reaching for her pack and then throwing it to her. "It's got all your

115

favorite foods in it again, just as earlier this morning. Plus, I added some berry pies, just for luck."

Alynia caught the pack with one hand, slinging it over her shoulder. She looked down and saw the sacred feathers of Nabu beneath one of the pack folds.

"Lucky feathers, too," she observed, winking at her mother and father.

She waved goodbye to them as she approached the nearby tree line, choosing not to make a big production about her departure, because the villagers were still celebrating, cheering, and dancing. She didn't want to say goodbye to Poplin or Frumpy, because she knew she'd end up crying in front of everyone.

As she walked into the woods alone, she began to cry anyway. She was glad that no one could see her. She walked for several hours in the night, comforted that she could still hear her village celebrating in the distance, but by midnight, when she decided to make camp, the thunderous chirping of the crickets drowned the music.

"Tomorrow, I'll be at Teetering Rock," she said to herself, stretching under the stars. Each star glimmered and twinkled at her as if they wished her luck on her journey. "Tomorrow, my destiny begins!"

Alynia closed her eyes, falling asleep under the cloudless sky.

## Author's Note

Once upon a time I went to a bookstore and something profound happened, I was inspired to create a strong female character. Over the years several people helped me keep my dream alive, to them I give thanks.

This spring when I woke up with the *now or never* attitude to get the book finished, something miraculous happened, the right people kept coming along at the right moments. The entire year feels like a magical dream and I'm still feeling the effects of its haze. Alynia Sky is my gift to the world, and I couldn't have done it without the love, support, and talents offered to me by friends and family. This truly was a team effort.

To my second family at

I couldn't have done it without your support.

I find myself overwhelmed with gratitude. Thank you all so much!

The adventure continues summer 2014

# Galactic Phoenix

Your dreams are beautiful and the world craves them, so please let them come out to play.